Prologue - The Beginning of the End

February 9th, 1938

Remember Lei, darkness is not the absence of light, it is the absence of you – Xian Taia

My mother had given me this notebook 6 years ago for writing stories. It already had the chapters printed on it. I received it just before she disappeared. This notebook is one of the only things left of her.

She had embarked on a mission involved with the on-going 'Second Sino war' or otherwise known as World War 2 in the West. She has never returned until this day. I was hoping that something of my mother's whereabouts would show itself. Although, none were revealed to me. I had spent days, flicking through the pages with no real purpose... Out of desperation? Grief? Wonder? Then it appealed to me.

This is a story of my life...

Chapter 1

Cast Away

I just stepped off the tram on the way to my aunt's lodge from school. I was in a rush because my friends and I were revising for our exams in the nearby park when I had lost track of the time.

I had barely knocked the door of my aunt's house and it was answered immediately. "Lei! You have no idea how worried I've been!"

I looked at her, there was an expression of worry on her kind face.

"Sorry auntie, I lost track of the time when we were revising in the park"

"Lei, please be more careful; you know the Japanese have shifted their patrol times in some areas. At least you are safe. Come inside, there's something I need to tell you"

My auntie was 14 when she had started supervising me since my mother went missing. I needed it, that comfort and that happiness which sheltered me. Even though she was young, for six years her protection had never faltered to this day.

I went inside to the living room and saw a man sitting there. You could tell that he was very powerfully built, just by looking at him. "Auntie, who is he, what is he doing here?". She blushed ever so slightly, I looked questioningly at her; strange really because I had never actually seen this reaction from my auntie before. "Lei this is Jiao Xu, he used to be my best friend when we were little. Sadly, my godmother, Liang Shu has broken her leg, and needs care, so my friend has come to take me to Hengsha Island", my aunt's voice hinted with guilt. "So, you will not be seeing me until December".

She turned to the man, "Jiao this is my niece Lei". The man nodded and smiled with sympathy. "We will be leaving tonight Lei, tell your father that I have moved to Hengsha".

"Auntie, please don't leave me with my stepmother by myself!"

"I have to, Lei, I don't have a choice. But you be careful around her now, especially when I am not here" she hesitated, "if...if you ever need to go somewhere, you might consider the market by that park".

I was so confused about why my aunt was suggesting me about going to the market. She saw my expression and continued "If you are ever in need of help, go to the market... you'll know when you need to. **Remember, Lei, darkness is not the absence of light, it is the absence of you**"

My auntie had left for Hengsha Island with Xu Jiao that afternoon and I returned outside my house's blue-grey door with a panel of glass by the side of it. I felt the shell-shaped brass knocker on the door which I had always loved the extremely accurate detail of it. I knocked.

A maid opened the door and looked at me with a hint of worry in her face. She pursed her lips and stated without expression, "Miss Xian, your mother is waiting for you in the living room". I hated the way the maids had been asked to speak to me, plainly and without expression.

My stepmother just kept trying to oppress me in whatever way she could. A few weeks ago, she heard the maids laughing and joking with me and she had got rid of that too. 'Just what is her objective? What is she going to get from doing this?' I asked myself. I never knew. It was just for her own entertainment probably. 'I'll conclude at that, there is no point in trying to find out'.

I put my bag down, held my head high and walked towards the living room. The maid opened the door to reveal my stepmother sitting on the leather couch clad in jewels, her expensive perfume filled the air and made my eyes and nose sting.

My stepmother lazily waved her hand to signal that the maid could leave. The door closed, she turned to me.

"Where have you been?" she screeched. Her cold, shrill voice echoed and seemed to drill into my head.

"My aunt's house" I replied plainly.

"Don't you dare be smart with me! Why are you late?"

"My aunt said she was moving to Hengsha Island tonight"

"So? that doesn't explain why you are late! Your aunt is a selfish person. She has kept you only to whisper behind my back, didn't she?" she whispered menacingly. I felt my face grow hot and said something which I had the urge to say for a very long time, it slipped out, "Never insult my aunt, the only person who deserves to be called that, is you!" I said firmly.

My stepmother had lost her temper too. She got up and slapped me on my cheek as hard as she could. I staggered under the force of the blow "How dare you!" she shrieked. Her long nails had cut my cheek badly.

I wiped my cut with my sleeve and I felt her cold, soft hands close around my wrist. She pulled me towards her as her long nails cut into my hand. I struggled in her vice-like grip. I kicked her shin as hard as I could. She shrieked in pain and let go, I snatched my hand back and saw the long scratch marks on it.

A moment later my stepmother, "I'm going to tell your father that you behaved like a wild animal!" |She sneered.

As my Niang left the room I felt like running, but my legs were frozen.

A few minutes later I heard, which I assumed was, my father thundering down the stairs. I dreaded what would happen.

"Lei! Is what your mother telling me true?!" he thundered.

I held my gaze defiantly.

"How dare you kick your mother!" he said, ignoring the scratches on face.

"But she slapped me!"

"Nonsense, she is your mother!"

Anger steadily rose in me again until I could hold it in no more. Then more words came tumbling out, "No! She is not my mother, and never will be!"

There was a slight pause, then his voice boomed through the house "Out! Get out!" And he lifted me by the back of my collar, got my schoolbag, and threw me outside and slammed the door behind me.

There I was out on the dark, dangerous streets of Shanghai. I felt a swoop of panic in my stomach. 'What should I do? Should I knock the door and ask for forgiveness? No, that was not an option to me.

Then amid my panic I heard a gentle voice in my head of my mother telling me something, it was a vague memory. **'Darkness is not the absence of light; it is the absence of you'**.

I had always believed in that, always tried to live up to what she told me.

'Ok, think straight, where is a safe place to go? My aunt has gone, wait, didn't she tell me something... the market, I think I know where to go' I thought.

Chapter 2

Unknown Allies

I had no fleece of any sort and although my uniform was made from cotton, it was still cold. But I ran to the market as fast as I could, trying to avoid recent Japanese patrol area.

As soon as I reached the market, I had to stop for I had no such stamina because I was used to riding in trams or in my father's car. I looked around the busy market, now the working-class citizens would be shopping after their long shifts.

"Hey! It is not safe for children here at this time of night!" called a voice from the midst of the crowd. I was not even sure if this person was talking to me. So, I started searching frantically for the speaker. But I could barely see more than 2 meters ahead of me.

"Come here child!" said the voice firmly.

As I was looking round for the owner of the voice, I felt a warm hand on my shoulder. This person had a firm grip and pulled me out of the crowd into a small teashop. The woman gestured kindly for me to sit down. As I sat down, I noticed this woman's features. She was around the age of

50 years and looked quite strong. Her face showed signs of age, but she had a kind look.

"What are you doing out here at this time child?" she asked. "You look tired and worried! Has something bothered you?"

I hesitated and lied "I was just coming to the market to buy something for my dad".

"This is no time for shopping now, with the Japanese patrolling the area at this time" she said softly. "What is your name?" she asked.

"Xian Lei" I replied, wondering if it was right telling my real name.

"Do you know Xian Jia Li?"

I nodded and said, "I am her niece".

A sudden excitement lit up in her kind face and she said as if she was bursting to say "Really! What a small world! My friend's goddaughter's niece you are!".

She looked so happy at this news and she finally said to someone else in the shop.

"Kai! Come here!" and immediately a boy about a year or two older than me, tall and muscular (who I assumed was an athlete) with messy black hair, dark green eyes which had a strong, kind gaze, came so fast I could have sworn that she summoned him by magic.

"Lei, I am Xu Nuo, call me Grandma Xu." She said, I nodded in response. I kept noticing that Kai had a lot of patience as Grandma Wu explained her name and what she teaches at her academy, calligraphy, painting, ancient studies, music and a range of martial arts.

"...And this is Kai" she said gesturing towards him. He smiled at me as she did so. "One of my students" She added. "Kai, this is Lei, my best friend's goddaughter's niece!" She cheerfully said.

"Hi Lei! Nice to meet you" said Kai, passionately.

"So, Lei, tell us why you are here at this time" asked Grandma Xu

So, then I began explaining that my aunt had to go to Hengsha Island and what happened at my house and what happened with my stepmother. It was a very uneasy topic to discuss with two people I had just met. But since I sort of knew Grandma Xu, I told them the truth.

I finished my explanation and I tried to keep my expression neutral, but Kai noticed a hint of sadness in my tone and expression. He looked me in the eye gently and reassuring said "Lei, don't worry, you are among friends". Grandma Xu looked at me and said "Lei, can you come to our academy tonight and then we will see if your parents want you home or not. How about that?".

"If that's fine with you, I'd love to come! Thank you so much!" I said gratefully. My thoughts jumped to what my mother had said 'The market really was the right place to go. Did my auntie know Grandma Xu? She probably did and maybe that's why she had told me'.

Chapter 3

XianXu Academy

Me, Kai and Grandma Xu took a tram to the academy. It was a welcoming building on a cherry blossom tree-lined street with cobbled lanes and glowing lanterns hanging from the buildings. This was a beautiful lane, unlike the one which I lived in, with concrete everywhere. This was like stepping into a different world.

"Welcome to our home" announced Kai spreading his arms wide as Grandma Xu opened the door. I saw a small hall (probably for teaching I thought) and I could also hear chatting and laughing coming from one of the other rooms. My question was soon answered. Grandma Xu lead me into the kitchen and I saw two boys in there, one chopping vegetables and the other wrapping meat, spice and vegetables in a dough. They were making dumplings.

'Wow!' I exclaimed in head, looking around the place.

"Who is this?" asked one of the boys in a curious voice.

"This is Lei Xian" replied Kai.

"Lei is staying with us overnight, longer if needed" said Grandma Wu.

Trying not to seem shy because I wasn't, I had learnt to be quite boisterous because of how my stepmother had treated me.

"Hi Lei" said one of the boys cheerfully. This boy had a dark messy brown hair that if you looked at it by itself it looked black, but next to Kai's head it looked brown. He also had brown eyes under his glasses. "I am Marat, nice to meet you!". He seemed to be as friendly as possible to me, I could tell.

"Hello Marat" I said happily. I noticed when I caught his eye, he winked at me. 'I am in good hands' I said to myself.

"Hello Lei" said the other boy. He had the same black messy hair, but he had piercing grey eyes that when he looked at me, I felt as if I was being x-rayed. "I am Jian". He spoke simply.

"Hi Jian" I replied.

"How-"

"Now that you have introduced yourselves, I think you children should eat and then sleep well, then you can talk in the morning." interrupted Grandma Xu, chuckling slightly.

The meal that the boys had made was better than anything I had eaten at home. The taste was beyond what Father's cook could do. Maybe home-made cooking really was amazing as all my friends would say at school.

"How did you learn how to cook like this?" I said in awe after we had finished our meal.

"My mother taught me" said Jian. "What about your mother, doesn't she cook?" After this question, silence fell between Grandma Xu and Kai. Jian and Marat (who was chatting to Kai) obviously noticed that something was wrong.

"Jian, my mother went missing when I was 6 years old, so I haven't really had the chance to learn to cook from her" I said simply, smiling. They all looked a bit shocked at my flawless reply.

"Then you can learn with us if you want" suggested Jian.

"I would love to, if it's not too much trouble".

"Not at all!"

"Thanks so much!"

Then Grandma Xu muttered.

As we all got up from the table, full and sleepy. "At dawn meet me down in the kitchen at 5:00am, sharp" Grandma

Wu said firmly, making me jump slightly. 'At 5:00! I normally woke at 6:00!' I thought.

"Lei, come with me for 5 minutes or so, I can patch up those cuts for you" said Grandma Xu

Pulling myself back to the present Grandma Xu said "Boys, after Lei comes, go and show her the music teacher's room". In response they all nodded happily and entered the corridor. That led out of the kitchen to the back of the building.

Grandma Xu took a box from a shelf and took a roll of a bandage. She cut it and stuck it on my cheek. Then I looked at my hand, the skin around the scratches were red and swollen. "She gave you a hard time didn't she" said Grandma Xu, examining my hand.

I smiled grimly. She went to the sink and got a bowl of cold, purified water, "keep your hand in here, then we can clean it and put a bandage on. When my hand had been cleaned with a rather saponaceous ointment Grandma Xu cut a length of bandage and gently wrapped it around my hand.

"Thank you" I said holding up my hand to see the bandage.

She smiled, "No problem, come, the boys will show you your room".

Grandma Xu led me to the boys' room. They showed me around the room that they all shared. It was a square room and there were three beds, each one against their own wall. The back wall had a window above the bed there.

Then they showed me my room. It was smaller than their room, but it gave me shelter. It had a window with opaque pale red curtains with music notes on them; "A music teacher had this room before you and she decorated it" explained Marat. A simple wooden desk sat below the window and a single bed with matching dark red sheets was next to the desk. A dressing table with single wardrobes on either side of it leaned against the walls.

Chapter 4

Home at last

I felt like I was home at last. A place where people thought well of me, helped me and more importantly, they showed that they considered me as family.

I loved writing stories. So just before I go to bed, I add something to them every night until they are finished. I washed myself and changed. Then I sat down on the chair and began writing on my desk, adding to this book, this story. All my previous stories started with some tale that my mother had told me and then I would build up on it. My mother had a taste for it.

I was just thinking of the vague memory when Kai came in.

I snapped from my daydream, "You still up?" I asked.

"That was what I was going to ask you" said Kai.

"What's Jian and Marat doing?"

"Well, Marat is sketching, as usual and Jian is trying to write a story for his assessment in school-"

"-A story?" I exclaimed

"Yeah, why are you so surprised?" he asked

"well, I am quite fond of story writing, in fact I'm writing a story right now"

"Ok, would you like to help him?"

"Sure! I'd love writing stories anytime!"

"That's great! He has been struggling to think of an appropriate story for so long"

"Really? I never knew writing stories was difficult" I said, 'How do some people found it so hard?' I asked myself. I shrugged, "Maybe I just have the talent" I said, rewriting my sentence. A sudden thought overcame me, "Kai, why are you here?"

"What do you mean?" said Kai, looking slightly confused.

"I mean, why do you stay overnight? Do you live in Shanghai? Are you a boarder?" I asked gently because I didn't want to offend him accidently. But Kai didn't reply. After a while he hesitated and said, "Are you sure you want to hear?"

"You don't have to tell me if you don't want to Kai" I said kindly, catching his eye.

"You have a way of listening that makes me want to tell you, and plus, I should learn from what you did at dinner." he said with an encouraging tone "As long as you don't tell anyone!" he said with a cheeky smile.

"I will never tell anyone because you gave me shelter. So, I will return the kindness." I said with a confident gaze.

He looked me in the eye and said "ok, I'll tell you".

"So, my mother was Chinese, and father was American. He worked for a bank in China and that is where he met my mother. They moved to China, near the harbour. When I was little, I used to ride my scooter with my parents by the docks and counted how many Japanese navy boats were docked there. One day there was something on the radio that my dad got really worried about and we didn't ride my scooter that day. We just stayed in the house and moved tables and chairs in front of the entrances and then pulled the shutters down.

That night we could hear the door smash open and my mother hid me under the bed and told me to be quiet, she ran to the phone and called Grandma Wu, yes-" he said looking at my confused expression "-I had been enrolled for classes at the academy. My mother was speaking in a worried tone which in turn made me worried. The house was being broken into as there was confusion everywhere. And then we saw the people who broke into the house were Japanese soldiers and they were armed.

They started shouting at my mother and father. My parents couldn't understand what they were saying but my mother was pleading." Kai stopped, then he sat down on my bed, buried his face in his hands and continued "They started beating my mother then my father grabbed the stick off them and started beating them". Kai paused. He hesitated, "And then they shot him", I gasped. I imagined that happening to my parents, it is horrible to see my father being shot in front of me.

I ran over to the bed and sat next to Kai and decided to change the subject "Let's go to your room and help Jian." I said kindly. His face was still buried in his hands. I closed my hand around his wrist and pulled gently. His hands came free he avoided my gaze and stared at the floor. "Come let's go" I said softly, smiling.

"Hey, what you have experienced is beyond what I can imagine. Everyone has feelings and there is no shame in showing them" I gave a sympathetic gaze.

We went to their room and there was Jian sitting upside-down against the wall. He was frowning in concentration as he held his schoolbook in front of his face. Marat was sitting on the floor, drawing something, "Hi Lei! Come sit down" and I sat down next to him, "What are you drawing?"

"It's an Azure-Winged Magpie-"

"It's a type of magpie species scientifically categorized as the Cyanopica Cyanus, they are able to inhabit and adapt with the Eurasian climate" interrupted Kai,

"Must you know everything about every single animal?" teased Marat.

"Does the bird really have blue wings. And do they really have a pitch-black head?"

"Yes, they do. Azure is also a shade of blue, that's why it's called an Azure-Winged Magpie"

"They do.", I looked at the pencil, slowly working its way across the page. Strokes so subtle yet the details so bold. No doubt that art is a talent, one that you are born with, gifts that only some can control.

Jian trying so hard to concentrate, "I think I should help Jian" I chuckled, and I turned around to Jian, "Sit the right way round and I'll help you with your story"

"Really!?"

"Yes, I will"

"You're good at it right?"

"Definitely, English is one of my top subjects"

"Great!"

"Sit the right way up"

"Ok", and he backward rolled on to the floor,

"Why were you sitting like that?"

"It helps me concentrate" he shrugged.

"Ok..." I replied unsurely, "Well, anyway, the word 'untouched' could be replaced with 'unblemished' or 'pristine'" I suggested. After a good half an hour of working on it, it was a great story.

Meanwhile, Kai and Marat were doing some exercises, "Can I try?" I asked

"Sure, we'll show you", I was absolutely rubbish, I couldn't even touch the floor let alone do a single press up! I was really fed up with myself.

"How do you do such exercises!"

"Well, me and Marat have been attending this academy for 6 years now and Jian has been here for 2 years, so we are kind of used to them now" replied Kai, I sat down on the floor, "Who's the oldest?"

"Kai is 14 now but he is going to be 15 in August. I'm 13, so is Jian, but I'm older than him by 4 months" explained Marat.

"I'm 12, I'll be 13 in April, only a few months younger but a lot shorter! I think it's because I have never even given a thought about walking to places, especially to school, I always ride on trams or by car"

"Don't worry, if you stay longer you can do simple exercises first then increase the intensity!"

"I think that is what I'll do, if I go home, I'll continue the routine"

"Good. Why don't we read your story? "suggested Kai.

"That's a good idea!", and I ran to my room, and picked up the book.

I sat on the floor and leant against Jian's bed while Kai and Marat sat either side of me Jian lay on the bed above us

"...the battle had only just begun" and I ended the story.

We talked and laughed until Grandma Xu came at 8:00pm and just in time too, to say that it was best we go to sleep for a waking at 4:30am. "Goodnight! And thank you" I said, sleepily.

"Sleep well, and you're welcome" replied Jian

What a strange day! Two hours ago, I was hopeless and now for once I feel home.

Chapter 5

Shadows of the past

I woke so early in the morning that it was still dark. I kept wondering if yesterday was a dream. That I never went to the supermarket, I never met Kai, Marat and Jian. I sat upright in my bed turned the lamplight on. It was not a dream, it was real. I decided to investigate.

I got changed into my school uniform and put on a coat that Grandma Wu gave me, then I lit a candle. I started exploring the academy, I loved exploring when I was little but when Niang came I wasn't even allowed out of my room most of the time.

I came out of my room and I was facing the boys' room. If I turned left, there was a dead-end and so, I turned right. There was another junction left leads to the kitchen and right leads to... I wasn't sure where it led to. It was just dark, so I turned right and there was a door with beautiful patterns illuminated in the candlelight.

I opened it and saw a garden with bamboo lattices and tomato vines growing up them and lots of other vegetables and flowers. There was a sand pit for some reason. But my attention wasn't on that. I was looking at the moon, the full moon was bright in the sky. It was very beautiful and I appreciated the sky's features more than I did for I had never really looked at the sky. I never star-gazed before.

There was a wooden bench facing the lattices. I went and sat on it. It felt comforting just sitting there, watching a mother bird feeding her young. I noticed it was an Azure-Winged Magpie. I could recognize it because Marat had drawn it the evening before.

The sun started to rise. I decided to get back before the others noticed that I was gone. I had a feeling that Grandma Xu wakes up earlier than the boys.

When the boys woke up, they came into my room at 4:30am, assuming I was still asleep (They were surprised to see me awake and changed already). Then we chatted for a bit and proceeded to the kitchen.

Grandma Xu was there waiting for us in the kitchen. She smiled at me and asked, "Did you have a good sleep?"

"Yes! I did"

"I can see you have because you seem so energetic!" she said pleasantly. "Come boys, you need to show Lei how to cook! They were all competing to show me how to hold a knife, how to switch on the stove...

Grandma Xu was just sitting by the kitchen table reading a book, and sometimes laughing at the boys trying to tell me what to do.

Finally, we made a dish of tofu. 'This is the earliest breakfast I have ever had, and most delicious!' I thought because I normally had it at 7:00 and now it is 5:30!

We finished breakfast in 15 minutes or so. 'I wonder what we are going to do next with so much time left.'

"...now come to the garden" Grandma Xu had said. My heart leapt, the garden? 'Is she talking about the same garden that I am thinking of?'

Yes, it was. The garden looked very different at day; it was all vibrant in a way.

"Boys! Do your exercises!" Grandma Xu turned to me and said "Lei, if you are going to stay for longer it is best you do our routine, don't worry-" I was a little shocked when she said 'our routine' because the boys were doing exercises that were impossible for me to do! "-you will do it at a less intense level, once you have achieved that you can move on to another, until you reach your full potential! First you need to master 20 press ups, 20 sit ups and 20 squats." I was determined to get as strong as the boys. I had decided to do something additional to my workout; 'I will run to school, its only half a kilometer from here!'

And so, I did, I ran non-stop. Grandma Xu and the boys did not know this as I didn't tell Grandma Xu. The don't go to the same school as me. They go to an international school.

I was flat-out when I arrived. My friend (Ju Mei) said she was worried because she rides on the same tram as me and I was not there.

"Lei! Where were you? You weren't on the tram." She had said to me at the school gates.

"My fa- I mean our chauffeur drove me" I lied because I didn't want her to be suspicious of my sudden desire to run to school. Yet Ju had noticed something different; 'maybe because I'm exhausted...''

In our 2-hour lunch break I went to the gym and started doing part of my work-out.

'School passed quite quickly today, what a relief!' I said to myself as I ran home and when I neared my house, I remembered that my destination wasn't there. It was at the academy. As I turned left away from my home, I yearned for my father to think well of me. 'Father, he was the one who kicked me out, why should he take sides with that woman! And not his own daughter!'

Chapter 6

Memories

But there is a bright side of being kicked out because I would never have met Kai, Marat and Jian. I also would never have learned how to cook or get stronger! I decided not to dwell on the thought of being neglected and think about this, pleasant thought.

As I reached the academy around 6:15pm, I found Grandma Xu cooking in the kitchen.

"Hello Lei, did you have a good day at school?" asked Grandma Xu.

"yes...I had...a great day!" I panted.

"Why are you looking so exhausted?"

"I ran here...from school".

"Wow! Really, I am happy that you are trying hard to get stronger" she said proudly. I just smiled back in appreciation. "Go and wash yourself and come back for dinner"

"Ok Grandma Xu!", I said gratefully.

After I showered, I changed into the spare clothes, Grandma Xu had given me and went down to the kitchen.

As I was helping Grandma Xu chop vegetables around 6:30pm, Marat came in.

"Why were you late." asked Grandma Xu, mockingly.

"Sorry Grandma Xu, I stayed for the Self-Study sessions so I could have more time to finish my English assessment" He looked at me and I smiled back. I was confused at this news. 'Aren't Marat and Jian in the same class? Shouldn't they both have had the assessment?'

"Why do you look confused?" He asked me.

"Oh, I was just thinking why you didn't get the assessment the same time as Jian", He smiled at me.

"Me and Jian are in different classes, he just had the assessment two days before me, that's all!"

"Oh...ok!" I said cheerfully "I'll help you!"

Soon after tea me and Marat went and sat down in his bedroom, I noticed he had a picture of who I thought was his mother and father. There was a strange candle holder with 9 branches; 'but it looked kind of delicate but that's not quite the word for it, maybe more elegant'. I thought.

"Kai told me you were Jewish" I said to him as I rubbed out his sentence.

"Yes, I am, so what?" he said mildly

"So, nothing just saying...What is that?" I said, facing my head toward the candle thing.

"Oh, that's a Hanukkiah, it's a Jewish candleholder for a celebration called Hanukkah"

"Really? What do you do on the day of Hanukkah?"

"Actually, it is eight days long" he said with a laugh and so he explained what Hanukkah was and then we just talked about our backgrounds and did our routine until Jian and Kai got home, at 7:00pm.

Two days passed and every night I would go to that garden because there was something familiar about it. At every night the truth seemed almost in my grasp but not quite. There I would gaze at its moonlit beauty, trying to find out something but I didn't know what.

On the third night a crescent moon was enlightening the garden. I hadn't heard her come.. "Come back again Lei?" said Grandma Xu's gentle voice, even though she talked softly, I was scared out of my wits!

"G-Grandma Xu? How did you know that I come here?"

"I come here myself to be bewildered by its beauty" she chuckled. "But also, to come and learn the truth, as you have been doing" she said explicitly.

"How did you know that I knew something about this place"

"-but can't remember what?" she interrupted, smiling. "I know this place is familiar to you, I think you saw this garden in a picture. Am I right?"

"Yes! The picture I used to have of my mother and auntie were younger sitting-" I hesitated "sitting over there?" asked Grandma Xu, pointing to the Lacebark Elm which grew behind the garden compound. "This garden was the foreground of the picture!" I hesitated and said, "How did you know?"

Grandma Xu came and sat next to me, "Your mother, her sister, who was your auntie and my son used to play here when they were children, in your mother's house.

Yes, this is your mother's house! But it has been converted and extended. The reason you had a place to go when your father kicked you out was because of your mother. Back then, called Ku Taia, she was one of the best Kung Fu students I had ever taught. After her marriage she was Xian Taia. She and my son, Xu Jiao (otherwise known as Master Xu) set up this place therefore it is called XianXu academy" she smiled a sadly. At this news I felt but there was still a flaw in my understanding, "How did she die?"

"You were six years when this war started and when your mother died." I nodded and Grandma Xu went on, "She was brave, she wanted to help make your world better so when our agents reported that Japan was planning to bomb Chongqing. Your mother told me that she was going with my son and few others to stop or at least delay the bombing so you and your father could escape and so could other citizens of Chongqing." Grandma Xu looked at me sadly and continued "Finally she only managed to delay it. My son and a few others came back but your mother was not amongst them. They had no idea where she was, but she saved your life. It broke your father's heart to leave you motherless."

"Where did she disappear?"

"There was a distress code sent to our base from somewhere in the Tibetan mountains, we tracked the signal as best as we could...but there was a snowstorm and we lost track of everything!"

Chapter 7

Tai's Letter

Few weeks passed, and a poster sent by Marat's sister, Cheng Tai, arrived. It was a poster to announce that all clocks must be changed to Tokyo time.

We were all sitting by the kitchen table.

"Why would Tai send us something like this?" asked Jian in a befuddled tone.

"Don't worry. I know Tai. She is clever and she must have written a message" Grandma Xu said. As she did, she examined the poster and her expression suddenly turned to as though she had just realized something.

She went to get something and she said to herself "Maybe she did this!" Barely after she said 'this' she wielded a hot iron box. We all looked open-mouthed at her as she held the iron barely an inch away from the paper some part of the paper started turning a brown-black colour.

"Grandma Xu, you're burning the paper!" I exclaimed.

"Watch, wait and see" she said simply in response. We all stared at her as if she had gone mad. "Look! I was right she has written a message without detection!" exclaimed Grandma Xu in a whisper. Four of us leaned closer for a better look. The letters were in brown-black colour. But Grandma Xu hadn't burnt the paper.

"Wow!" whispered Marat marveling at his sister's cleverness.

This is what the letter said,

To Marat,

I am captured in Bridge House, the second floor in the fourth cell and I am the chief's personal translator. I am going to try and develop a friendship with him, naturally. Further news is that I have met four Chinese citizens in prison who claim to be Grandma Xu's friends. They were apparently helping her to delay the bombing of Chongqing, years ago. They have been beaten brutally and they have to sit cross-legged on the floor. There is barely enough space for them all to lie down. They even get punished if they lean against the walls. Their names are, Liu Zhen, Liu Tu, Zhou Fen, Chen Li.

Are these people your allies Grandma Xu?
Do not risk writing back and I hope you're all safe. Be wary that there are spies in the even in the unlikeliest of places. Be careful about who you trust. I hope that I will see you soon.

Your sister,
Cheng Tai.

Marat's expression was filled with horror, "Grandma Xu! We have to help them, fast!".

"It's alright Marat, your sister is strong she will be alright", as I sat next to him, I remembered something, "But Grandma Xu, are those people your allies?"

"I almost forgot, let me check" she murmured all the listed names to herself and suddenly said "Yes! They were the lost part of the troop when they went to delay the Japanese!"

I went sort rigid and said "Wait! Give me the letter!" I went through the names; Liu Zhen, Liu Tu, Zhou Fen, Chen Li.

No, my mother's name wasn't on there. "But not all of the missing ones are here" I said wistfully. The boys looked confused at my tone. However, Grandma Xu noticed what was wrong. She kneeled next to me and whispered kindly. "Do you want me to tell them?" I thought about it and said "Ok".

Grandma Xu stood up and said sadly "Lei's mother, Xian Taia, and my son, Jiao Xu, were the founders of this academy; therefore, its name is XianXu academy. Her mother was also part of the squadron that set off to delay the Japanese bombing. They succeeded but Lei's mother was not among those who returned" the boys looked horrified at this and they all tried cheering me up for the next hour or two.

"Don't worry Lei! We'll find her" said Jian encouragingly. Then Kai sat down next to me, "Lei, you should be proud of your mother. we would never have had a home. We would never have met each other and you would not have had a roof over your head at this time" I nodded in response.

"It's funny how one choice can do so many things" I said thoughtfully, "Like if I push you off the bed" as I said so I pushed Kai off the bed and (fortunately, for me) Marat was lying on the floor, below the bed (staring at the ceiling), and you know what happened. As Kai fell on him, me and Jian burst out laughing until our tummies hurt. At that moment Grandma Xu opened the door and she found them in a heap on the floor and she started laughing too!

After we had calmed down Kai said "You have become really strong"

"Thanks!" I agreed. Almost two months had passed since I had met them and I had moved on to the next level of intensity.

The next day we all measured our height. I had grown about 2cm since my arrival. "I am so proud of you Lei; I think you are now ready to start training your reflexes"

"Thank you, Grandma Xu", I was so happy. Finally, I had come to a level where I could start training my reflexes with a moving opponent.

She looked at me with a warm smile. "You look so much like your mother when I told her she was ready. You have her courage, her kindness and her taste for stories" she hugged me and left.

To hear my mother's character being told from someone who knew her well, it was the value of gold to me. My mother seemed like a nice person.

She was part of me, yet she seemed so distant...

Chapter 8

Hengsha Island

3 days later still no news from home. However, that day Grandma Xu had gone to the market.

Grandma Xu came back with terrible news; "Lei! Do you know what is happening?" I rushed out of my room to the kitchen, "What?"

"There are 'missing' posters of you everywhere! And anyone who finds you gets a reward of 1 million yuan!"

"What!"

"Yes! I know"

"So, my father is trying to buy me back?!" I was so angry at him, 'why can't he come back to get me himself? After all, I sent him a letter of where I was!'

"Lei, I think the best option is to go back to your father. He misses you. He has even got the whole of Shanghai to look for you!" she suggested gently.

"No! I'm never going back. He knows where I am, if he wants me home then he can come and get me himself!" I turned my back on Grandma Xu and folded my arms. She sighed "Do you really want to stay away from him?"

"Not from my father, but from my stepmother, she won't let him show that he cares for me or even show any emotion towards me. He is basically her puppet. If he wants me to come home, he has to get rid of her first!" I said stubbornly

Grandma Xu sighed and put a hand on my shoulder said "I was planning to go to Hengsha Island as it my turn to take the months' shift of deactivating Japanese torpedoes, I suppose I can bring forward that date and we can stay permanently" she said looking me in the eye.

Then all the boys tumbled through the door...

"Lei they put posters-"

"-of you! -"

"-everywhere-"

Then they saw our expressions and they all smiled sheepishly at me and Grandma Xu.

"We are moving permanently, to Hengsha" explained Grandma Xu.

"What?!" they all said at the same time.

"We need to escape otherwise the police will be looking for Lei in a few days"

"Uh, Grandma Xu? Why can't we go to Changxing instead? It has more guerrillas on the Allied side" asked Kai

"Good question, what we have to be careful of is not to reveal too much information to anyone, not even our agents, just in case of betrayal. So, we must act like common citizens, because it will be suspicious for us to be in constant protection of guerrillas", she replied

"When do we leave?" asked Marat.

"Tomorrow, at the crack of dawn", we nodded and went to pack our possessions.

"Lei! What happened?" exclaimed Jian.

"I just- I just want them to leave me alone! He is forcing me to come back home! And first he should get rid of that horrid woman, he knows I hate her!" I whispered angrily as I stuffed my possessions in my schoolbag.

"Let's- let's take our eyes of that topic. Lei you know, me and Marat, we used to go to Hengsha to play with the dolphins, a woman called Xiu Liang would show us some tricks with them. There are two dolphins we named Zhen and Zhu and they are awesome!" explained Kai.

"Wow! Really? That sounds amazing" I said, 'it sounds almost otherworldly to play with dolphins and I had never seen the sea, I had only seen pictures of their fins poking out of the waves'.

We all ate quickly and slept early for a waking at 3:00am the next day.

I snapped upright at the sound of Grandma Xu waking up the boys next door.

"Come on, we have to go before the rush hour starts". I was half-asleep, when I got up and walked into the opposite wall.

"W-What? Oh, ok I'm up" I yawned. I dressed quickly and snatched my bag from the floor.

"Come on!" and we were shoved out the door by Grandma Xu then we started making our way to the shore. It was so quiet, a few people out on the road lit up by a few lanterns I had never been outside at 3:30am.

It was 6:00am and we had almost reached the shore, but we were all hungry since we had eaten no breakfast. So, Grandma Xu ordered a quick lunch of stir fry noodles and a few rolls of sweet bread.

Finally, we reached shore! Grandma Xu had rented a small sampan boat to travel to Hengsha Island. After a while we stopped chatting and started looking at the sea, it was almost like magic for me, seeing it for the first time.

But then something went wrong; 'the boat is at a stand-still, this is terrible!' Just then Kai pulled out his flute and started playing, it sounded like a plea for help, except in a musical language.

Then two blue-black shapes cut were swimming towards the boat, 'it's going to hit us!' I screamed inside my head. Marat started splashing the water playfully. And the two shapes leapt out of the water, "they are dolphins?" I exclaimed. "Wow!" I turned around saw Kai his eyes bright with happiness, but he kept playing and this time the tune changed slowly to a playful mood.

"Stop playing, we need help!" said Grandma Xu, pointedly.

"They are not playing Grandma Xu, look!" I said. Because Marat had put two life buoys that were tied to the boat in the water and the dolphins were making gentle clicking noises.

"Why are they doing that?" I asked Marat.

"That is how they find stuff, like the rubber ring for example. They use soundwaves that hit objects in the water, and then they detect those waves of sound that bounce back at them" he explained.

The two dolphins slipped into the rubber rings and started towing the boat at break-neck speed.

And soon enough there were two splodges of green lumps on the horizon "The island, I see the island Grandma Xu!"

"Yes! Well done Lei! We'll be there by around 6:00pm, I've contacted an agent to meet us there then we can see where we can stay.

Finally, the island, we're here! It was beautiful place with not many houses. There were just hamlets and fields everywhere, greener than I could imagine. The people there were very kind and willing to help us with our luggage as if they were waiting for us all that time.

A fisherman was waiting at the docking bay, he and Grandma Xu were discussing in serious tones. We moved into a house with three bedrooms. My bedroom was moderate but convenient, it had a small sapphire orchid in a white porcelain pot on the windowsill. There were white curtains down to the floor. with pale blue lines randomly cutting across it, the floor was bamboo, a bamboo desk with drawers sat in a corner, a set of waist-high drawers was next to it, my bed was in the opposite corner to the desk had plain pale blue sheets. 'This is perfect!' I thought and there we washed ourselves and changed into the new clothes Grandma Xu had bought for us.

Chapter 9

January 14th

I woke up early in my new bedroom with a burst of happiness. I jumped out of bed and hurriedly combed my hair and got changed. It was January 14th.

I ran to the kitchen to find Grandma Xu cooking. But the boys were in a corner, talking in whispers, and when I came in, they all snapped up and looked at me in an expression that made me very suspicious.

"Just say it boys" chuckled Grandma Xu.

"Happy birthday Lei!" said Jian. Meanwhile, Marat and Kai had gone to get something.

"How did you know it was my birthday?"

"Well, we told Grandma Xu that your birthday is in January because you told us, and she sent a letter to your auntie and that is how we found out your birthday!"

Just then Kai and Marat came back holding a small package.

"Sit down" said Grandma Xu. I sat down on the floor and the boys sat down in front of me. The package was wrapped scruffily in a brown paper. "Open it" urged Kai and I opened the small package to reveal a thin rectangular leather box. I opened the lid of the box and a smooth black cylinder surface was nestled among black velvet lining. I pulled it out and it was a fountain pen with gold rimmed lid there was also an ink bottle with purple ink.

"My father never bought me anything like this for my birthday!" I was overwhelmed. I always wanted a fountain pen but all I got was useless dolls and shoes that I would never use. I think he doesn't even know what I even enjoyed.

"Wow! Thank you so much!" I said, "Why did you buy such an expensive pen for me?"

"Because you're like a sister to us, just like we are brothers to you!" said Jian.

Later that day my auntie, Xian Jia Li and Master Xu visited our house. "Auntie!" I exclaimed. She gave an expression of surprise and I ran towards her and hugged her. She started laughing and crying at the same time. "Happy Birthday, Lei!" she proclaimed with a hint of pride in her voice.

That evening I was sitting on the roof of our house watching the sun dip below the silhouette of the mainland.

"You ok?", I turned around to see Jia Li climbing onto the roof.

"I'm fine... just relaxing" I replied as she sat next to me.

"There is *something* on your mind, what is it?" she asked me, I hesitated for a moment,

"Where did my mother come from?"

"She was born in Jiang Xi" Jia Li replied slowly.

"I mean that... you know, she doesn't have a national name. 'Taia' it's... unusual, as if her name has had slight mutations"

"Ah, I know what you mean. You see, her name is a Tahitian name because her family came from Tahiti"

"Really! Her family is from the French Polynesia?" I uttered in surprise

"Yes, they are. Her forefathers are originally from China, but they immigrated there to find more agricultural land and because they loved exploring." Jia Li responded.

"But then why was my mother born here, in China?"

"I assume they were treated as lower-class citizens because the French had control over the Polynesia, so they probably decided to come here".

"That is quite a story" I said.

"You seem to have a lot of heritage!" she teased.

"It's very nice knowing that her heritage is combined with something else".

Chapter 10

The missing piece

We were cooking in our new home and I just asked Grandma Xu,

"Grandma Xu, can you send a letter to my auntie, Xian Jia Li?"

"Of course, you want to see her, in fact I am going to Xiu Liang's house. I presume your auntie is there. Why don't you come with me?"

"Yes please! I would love to come!"

"Let's go! -" she turned to the boys, "Boys! Lei and I are going to Xiu Liang's house, ok! If you go out then take the keys, I have the spare set with me anyway but just incase"

There was an indistinct 'ok' from another room.

We went by rickshaw to the beach near by her house and walked the rest of the way. There were lots of children playing at the beach and I noticed that there was my auntie playing with some children.

When she looked up, "Are you ok?"

"Yes"

"Why are you here?"

"Because-"

"Never mind, what about your father? I know he kicked you out-"

"-how did-"

"-Grandma Xu sent me a letter. What has happened now?"

"He has put 'missing' posters of me all over Shanghai"

"What?! He knows where you are. Why didn't he come and get you himself?"

"I don't know, but he doesn't know you are here" I replied.

"That's fine, let's send him a letter saying you have moved here with me, ok?"

"Ok!"

"Grandma Xu, thank you so much for looking after her!"

"No problem, she actually helped us too!"

"How can I pay you back?"

"No, no don't worry, no money needed. You told her the right thing", my auntie smiled.

"Jla Li?" said Grandma Xu, in a whisper.

"Yes?" Jia Li replied.

"Would you be kind enough to take this to Agent 0495?" she asked.

She received the slip of paper and said, "Is that all?" and Grandma Xu nodded kindly.

"Come, come inside!" as she led us to a little cottage with a big garden and lots of cherry blossom trees, chrysanthemum, peony and orchids. It was a beautiful house, like out of a story in one of my books.

We went inside and I saw an elderly woman sitting in a chair with her leg in a heavy cast. She was reading a book peacefully. The woman noticed us come in.

"Hello Jia Li and Xu Shun, my old friend!"

"Liang, are you well?"

"I am OK but finding it incredibly hard not being able to walk! Right now, I would be with the dolphins"

"Talking of dolphins, two of them towed us half of journey to here!"

"Really, I think those two are Zhen and Zhu. They would have the energy to and the most energetic twins anywhere they are!" she chuckled. She turned to me and said, "Jia Li, is this your niece?"

"Yes, this is Lei" replied my aunt cheerfully.

"Nice to meet you Lei" Liang said warmly, "I am Xiu Liang, but call me Grandma Liang. I have heard about your story from your auntie. Don't worry, you are welcome on this island. And I believe Kai and Marat are your friends, are they behaving?" she chuckled.

"Yes, they are mischievous though!" I said with a smile. All of them started laughing. And then, we all had dinner at Grandma Liang's cottage. I missed my auntie's cooking.

The next day we all got up early in excitement and rushed into the kitchen and ate breakfast quicker than usual.

"Children, we are going to the hospital today!"

"I don't want an injection!" screamed Marat, his face went white, Grandma Xu frowned.

"Did you just scream like a little girl?" I asked

"No... maybe" he squeaked.

"We will be going to the hospital today to visit Grandma Liang" she said pointedly to Marat who smiled sheepishly.

"Has she broken an arm now?" asked Kai.

"No"

"Another leg"

"No"

"The same leg?"

"No! She has just gone to check her already broken leg"

"Oh" we said in unison.

We travelled by rickshaw to the local hospital. It was a smaller version of the one in Shanghai. Grandma Liang's ward was on the ground floor and so it was easy to access. When I had arrived at the hospital, I saw that it had been built around the biggest redwood tree I had ever seen.

The ward doorway was literally a hole carved in base of the tree. I opened it and it was not what I was expecting. There was a tree and flowers, a window that faced the shore and it was beautiful. Certainly, it wasn't not like the concrete and plastic wards in Shanghai.

There was a nurse checking Grandma Liang's leg. A doctor opened the door of the ward in hurried manner and murmured to the nurse and the nurse gasped and clasped her hands over her mouth and ran over to the door to see something. The doctor was muttering in a serious tone. I caught one word that made my heart leap and sink at the same time: 'Taia'

The boys all looked at me "Go and investigate, even if she is not your mother! I think she will be very excited if you see her." Grandma Xu whispered in my ear. Then she looked at the boys, "Go with Lei" They nodded, and we followed the people who were about to leave.

They went in a lift to the third floor and we followed. Some people broke off the group which was pushing the bed and we saw the woman; she had taken some beating. She was in worn-out clothes; her shoulder had a deep cut and she had scratches on her cheek. The minor bandages that were put on her were blood-stained. She had obviously been hurt, severely. But under all her injuries she had a beautiful, kind face and she looked in her late 20's.

"Who are you? Children are not supposed to be here!" said the doctor who was pushing the bed.

"W-We are her uh, r-relatives" I stuttered uncertainly, he eyed us suspiciously to find any false truths. Grandma Xu appeared at the end of the corridor. "Wait! Doctor, I need to have a word with you!" They were talking in barely audible whispers.

Finally, the conversation ended the doctor turned to us, "Ok" he said.

"Wait out here though, until you can enter" he insisted, as he pushed the bed into a private ward. We nodded.

We looked through the glass in the doors, a team of medical staff were fitting a mask over her nose and mouth. They were getting bandages and medicines. I slid down the wall and crouched on the floor. I had buried my hands in my face. I couldn't look, if she was my mother then I wouldn't be able to stand being here. A nurse came out of the private ward and Jian suddenly asked her "Excuse me, what is that woman's name" he said indicating the person in the ward. The nurse jumped back in surprise for a moment and said "Oh, sh-she is Xian Taia"

"Ok, thank you" said Jian, looking at the ward. The nurse glanced at us uncertainly and left without another word.

"Looks like she is your mother" Kai said, gently.

"But even if she is, I don't know her. She is like a stranger to me" I whispered and my voice muffled from underneath my hands.

"Poor girl" exclaimed Grandma Xu "I hope she is alright."

"Grandma Xu, is this my mother?" I said, looking up at her.

"She does look like your mother, but I cannot tell that well because I have not seen her for 6 years" when she saw my disappointed face she added, "Don't worry, we can ask the reception for the ward matron's phone number" she said kindly, "and we can check her daily reports." That made my spirits lift slightly.

One more question tugged at me, "Grandma Xu, who was that doctor you were talking to?" I asked her.

"Xiu Liang told me that he was an agent she knew on this island, she asked me to go and speak to him.

The next week passed with no trouble and regular reports of Xian Taia showed that she was recovering well. Grandma Xu and my auntie were thinking of a plan to get the prisoners out of Bridge House without needing to fight the Japanese guard.

Meanwhile, Taia had been transferred by our agents to another field hospital in Tibet which was still in control of local people. As the Japanese still controlled Hengsha island and if they found out, they would punish the whole island severely.

In the meantime, we were attending a local school. I loved the extra things in subjects they do for example in biology.

We would go outside and counting how much giant pandas we can see and seeing how ants build new homes. This was all way much more fascinating than Shanghai.

It was late November, Grandma Xu had taken leave from our school to go to Nyingchi, Tibet. She wanted us to check if Taia was strong enough for us to take her to our home. Meanwhile, it would be a good training area for us, learning to adapt quickly to different environments; especially when it was cold. And for the first time, I had seen snow!

We stayed in a safe house mainly used for meetings and relaying information. It was very busy with agents coming and going.

At the end of the week the matron from the hospital informed us that Taia was now conscious. We ran to the hospital and found her sitting on the hospital bed. She was bandaged up and all her minor injuries tended to. She was sitting upright, reading a newspaper, with a rather confused expression.

When we came in, she looked at us, "Hello there" she said with a smile, her voice was soft and gentle. Her face looked younger and cleaner.

"Hello" I said, my voice cracking slightly.

"What shall I do for you?" Taia asked. I felt a tinge of sadness because she had not shown any sign of recognition but then, she had not seen me for 6 years.

"How did you end up like this?" asked Grandma Xu.

"You probably wouldn't believe me if I told you" Taia chuckled in reply.

"Please tell us, then we will not bother you?", insisted Grandma Xu, Taia pursed her lips unsurely. Only then, did a nurse come in and whisper something to Taia.

Finally, Taia looked back at us with a challenging gaze as the nurse left the room and closed the door. "You are staying at the safe house, aren't you?" she asked bluntly.

"y-yes, we are" replied Marat, a little shocked.

"Tell me the last message that had been passed last night, under the very same roof that you have stayed at. Otherwise, you will not be allowed out" Taia said, with a hint of a sly smile.

Uncertainty dawned on me, none of us had been at the house during the evening messaging shifts.

I looked behind me and saw the ward matron locked the door. I glanced at Grandma Xu whose expression was calm, she caught my eye and subtly shook her head.

There was something that could get us through this situation, I took this book from my back and opened the first ever page, 'that's it' I thought

"Remember, darkness is not the absence of light, it is the absence of you." I stated.

Her expression pacified and she nodded her head, "Very well" she replied. Taia let out a sigh and asked, "Are you sure you want me to tell you?"

"Don't worry, we are used to hearing strange adventures" said Grandma Xu.

"If you're sure" the woman said with a smile.

"Sure"

"Ok, well there was a bombing in Chongqing a few years ago. I went to the nearest hospital, but I lost my identity during the incident. So, I started making my way to a friend's house in Nyingchi and I sent a distress call to my friends with my remaining money, about six or seven years ago in Chengdu. I was trapped in the mountain ranges. My friends found me and brought to the Island, mainly because there were Japanese spies nearby and I got transported back here. They always have tentacles almost everywhere" she said with a smile.

"So uh, do you have any family members who live close by?" I asked.

"Well, to be honest I'm not really sure"

"Who are they"?"

"I don't think you will know them, but my husband, Xian Zhao and daughter Xian Lei escaped from the bombing, that's all I know"

"How old is your daughter?" I asked,

"um-" she said, in deep thought

"- I think she is about twelve to thirteen years old now" I interrupted

"Yes! How did you know?" she asked, surprised. My stomach swooped uncomfortably as I tried to smile. Grandma Xu looked at me and then back to the woman.

She froze, then stared at me and tears slowly came to her eyes.

"Lei? Is that you?" she asked, her gentle voice cracked. I nodded, and tears started to swell in my eyes. "You're all grown up" she looked at me, head to toe.

I ran and threw my arms around my mother. She was crying so much that my shoulder got wet quickly, but I didn't mind.

After a while she looked at my face and wiped my tears away, gently. She smiled at me and whispered, "I never thought you would be this grown up. I'm sorry, I couldn't watch you grow up"

"It's ok mama, you risked your life for me. Otherwise, I would never be here" She smiled at me and turned to Grandma Xu, I thought I could recognize you Grandma Xu! How is the academy?"

"Everything is alright Taia
, but we have lost many because most of them have gone to Chaozhou. But we have one more permanent recruit, Ming Jian" As she said so she motioned towards Jian.

"Hello Jian, how did you come to be at the academy permanently?" She asked

He flushed slightly and said, "It's a long story".

"Don't worry, you don't need to tell me" she said kindly, smiling.

"It's just that-"

"-It's ok, I understand, many people who come to the academy have different backgrounds and culture" then she said, "You can talk to me later. Lei, in a few weeks I will be able to go on a wheelchair, then I can keep up with you"

"Come, it's time to go" said Grandma Xu gently. "We can visit your mother until she can come home"

"Ok" I agreed, "Bye Mama"

Chapter 11

Bridge House

December passed quite quickly and my mother was making a slow but steady recovery. I would visit her every day and read her a story that I had written.

Finally, she was strong enough to go on a wheelchair, but she still could not walk. We took her back to Hengsha and the journey took almost a month. My auntie was so happy when she saw my mother in her house. Then they were both talking forever about their old memories.

At these times we would almost forget there was a war going on.

One day when me and the boys came back from the beach to find my mother and Grandma Xu talking in serious voices in the kitchen,

"... No, not Tai! She can't be there!" my mother sounded shocked.

"What are you talking about?" I asked.

"Bridge House. We are thinking of a plan to get the prisoners out of there." My mother replied with a confident smile.

"Can I see what you have done so far?"

"Of course! Well, we haven't done much so-"

"It's ok! I can also help, I'm great at planning out and spotting flaws!" My mother looked at me with an unsure expression. Grandma Xu added, "You should trust your daughter. She has talent to do this", I smiled with appreciation.

"Ok!" she agreed.

So, my mother, auntie and myself sat down and began rewriting and adding parts of the plan. Mama wasn't very good at planning, but she was good at coming up with ideas. Auntie was good at planning a little bit, "Maybe I haven't inherited all of my father's planning skills!" she chuckled.

The plan took 3 days and 3 nights to complete. Finally, it was done.

Grandma Xu called all the boys to come. Master Xu had come to visit us too.

When he came in my mother opened the door and he was so surprised, "No, she is not there! I am imagining things" he murmured to himself. My mother looked annoyed and my auntie had come to see what was taking so long. When she saw her best friend, she folded her arms, frowned and said, "What are you doing?!"

"She-" You are standing there for 10 minutes goggling at her!"

"But-"

"Yes! She is alive now come in!" While they were having this conversation, me and the boys were laughing so badly that we got hiccups at the end.

"Ok, calm down now, let us all hear the escape plan" said Grandma Xu as she pulled the bamboo shutters down and lit the candle, "Give me your plan" she said to me and I handed it over.

Throw a bag full of ropes, lattices and some gardening supplies (Because Tai had persuaded the Major General to make a garden and a small farm inside the prison so he could have all his favourite fruits, vegetables and meat for himself. The prisoners did the gardening and tending to the animals).

A lattice and a few ropes can be put against the prison walls (The prison windows have keys to unlock them for maintenance)

Tai must steal the keys when the prisoners are gardening that day (The guards would be celebrating New Year, and so will be Major General. If there are any guards on watch, they will be watching the prisoners).

We will park a maintenance van by the hotel at 478 North Szechuan Road, precisely at Midnight (We will give Tai a signal and she will distract any guards who are watching while the prisoners will use the lattices and ropes to climb over the walls along with herself).

Once they are inside the truck, we will provide them with Japanese uniforms (Tai will steal some). Then use false identity papers just in case.

Drive to the Yangtze river and board a small boat (with a lower deck to hide the prisoners just in case)

We proceed towards Hengsha Island via Yangtze river and go to a French Concession where one of our agent's house is and the prisoners can wash themselves and be treated. They can go to the academy with Master Xu while we go on ahead to Hengsha Island.

"Wow! This plan is great! Is it going to take place during the New Year?" asked Grandma Xu.

"Yes, so then the guards and Major General will be celebrating, this is what we coordinated with Tai"

"Good, you have thought of everything, even for us!" exclaimed Master Xu.

"Thank you, Master Xu!"

"Come on, let's start preparing, there is only 2 weeks left until February 13th!".

So, over the next few days we were stitching sacks, pouches, extra little things to our T-shirts, making holes in clothing and fraying it to make it look like a peasant's clothing.

Finally, it was ready. We started at 10:50pm boarding three small sampans paddled by some trusted agents who were fisherman and looked quite poor.

We reached mainland at 11:10pm. Master Xu gave them money as it was an act of kindness and it was New Year's Eve. Surprisingly the fishermen did not want the money but then Master Xu insisted. In the end the fishermen were very thankful.

I couldn't believe what we were going to do but this might change the course of history.

"Wait here, I'll go and get the truck" said Master Xu. Five minutes later we saw a maintenance truck heading our way. "Come, we have only half an hour to get there"

We got in the truck. It was quite spacious, but with five more people, I thought it would be a bit of a squeeze.

We got there at 11:50pm, we got delayed because of people getting ready to parade down the roads. The prison had a towering, estimated 80 ft compound wall and it smelt bad too.

The four of us children got out to check if there were any Japanese soldiers.

We poked our heads from the back of the van. It was exactly midnight; we heard a sudden uproar from the crowds that made me jump so badly; The New Year celebration had begun "That scared the life out of me! Anyway, it's clear" I whispered. We saw an indistinct face peek out of a barred window. Marat's face lit up and he gave a thumbs up to the figure.

"Is that Tai?" I asked.

"Yes!" He whispered with a smile.

We waited a while until we heard stifled grunts and clatters behind the dark, prodigious wall. Moments later five figures were clumsily climbing over the high prison walls, we hurled a rope ladder up to the prisoners. We all watched with our hearts beating in our throats willing them not to fall.

As they inched closer to the ground I could see their faces tight with concentration slowly on moving their shaking limbs steadily down the swaying ladder.

They climbed off the ladder and were helped into the van by Master Xu and my mother.

"Lei, can you check if there are any bystanders on the road?" asked my mother in a low whisper.

"Sure!" I replied as I peered down the isolated road, there was a faint sound of the celebrations of the New Year and they were getting closer. "There isn't anyone at the moment, but we will need to move because the celebrations sound like they are heading this way" I said with a hint of urgency.

"Ok, get in!" As soon as I got in Master Xu started driving.

"Xu Nuo! How nice to see you all again!" said a man to Grandma Xu.

"It's good to see you again. The woman who was sitting next to him looked at my mother, "Taia?! -"

"-I know, how am I alive isn't it? Well, I'll summarize it" she said "I sent a distress call in Chengdu after Chongqing got bombed. I got transported to Hengsha and here I am!", she said it simply and finished with a smile.

The prisoners stared at her as if she had gone mad.

"Anyhow, who is this, a new recruit?" a woman asked Grandma Xu.

"Actually, she is my daughter" said my mother.

"Really? She has grown so much since I have last seen her!", she smiled at me, "Hello!"

I turned to look at Tai. She was the same height as her younger brother and had the same round glasses, brown eyes and brown-black hair. In fact, they looked like twins. If Tai didn't have shoulder-length hair, then I could have sworn I was seeing double. "Hello" I said to Tai, but she avoided looking me in the eye and blushed furiously. I looked at Marat questioningly. He looked kind of embarrassed, worried or even regretful. He cast a sideways glance at his sister and said "Sh-she... th-the thing is, she can't talk, she has no voice"

I paused for a second 'a person without a voice? I've never heard of such things' I thought, "But, why didn't you tell me before?" I asked him

"Well, you see... lots of people have insulted her, not given her the proper treatment a normal person would have, so, I-I thought it would be better not saying anything"

"That's understandable and it's ok! I don't care if someone has a voice or not, they're still a person-" I paused "-I've been treated like that too, my father and stepmother have silenced my voice until I came here" I said. Tai looked up at me and smiled. I opened my mouth to say more then I was interrupted by people angrily shouting. Everyone fell quiet as we turned around a corner by a bamboo forest.

"Children, go outside and divert any Japanese in any way you can. Don't get hurt, keep in the Southwesterly direction" Grandma Xu whispered. I caught my mother's eye and she nodded and smiled at me, "Go, I think you are now capable of this" she whispered kindly. I nodded in response "See you soon" I whispered as I got out of the van. Tai climbed out too and looked at her brother, "Tai is coming too, she tells me she is capable of this" said Marat.

"Ok- now go!" said Grandma Xu.

Chapter 12

The Great Escape

The van drove away and no sooner had a Japanese patrol jeep had appeared on the scene than the boys climbed up the bamboo trees. They were ready with sling shots just in case, I would be there, with Tai to divert the Japanese to buy time for the prisoners to escape.

Two Japanese armed soldiers got out of the jeep and one pointed at me. I wanted to run, but I had a feeling that if I ran that would be the last time I would. I felt my heart beating fast against my ribs as they came closer towards me.

"You! Did you see anyone jump over that wall?" one of them said in an arrogant, demanding tone.

I kept my tone steady and said "Yes, I did"

"Where did they go?"

"They ran over to the lake, by the market", the soldiers looked at each other and ran over to the lake.

As soon as they were out of sight, I looked at Tai and she nodded confidently, the two of us ran, deeper into the forest, the boys leaping from tree to tree above me.

Then I heard shouts from behind me. "You lied! Filthy peasant!" The Soldiers had come back and were chasing after me.

I kept running blindly into the heart of the forest. At last, I reached a dense cluster where it felt like the forest was closing in on me from all directions. My heart was pounding. The forest was quiet and no sign of the boys anywhere but I had a strange feeling that we were not alone. The humid and damp atmosphere was suffocating. The bamboo stalks were so tall, they felt like giants. The two of us hid in the deepest part of the clusters and I let out a breath of relief.

"Over there!", This wasn't the soldiers but it a new voice and sounded like they had heard me. I lay still, half-hidden by leaves on the ground. "There is no point searching all those clusters, but I know a quicker way" said one of them.

Then I felt a deep swoop of fear and panic.

"Isn't that girl on the posters in the city?" a man asked.

"Yes, I think so anyway. But even so, that woman had said to catch her daughter and she would give us the reward money".

"We can keep the girl in our custody and ask for more money".

I soon realized that my stepmother had sent these people to capture me, but they were using me to blackmail for more money. I wasn't sure who these people were nor did I know that they were with the Japanese soldiers or not, even so, I was still in imminent danger.

"Over here" someone had said.

I whisked around and saw a man behind me, "Come here, we'll return you to your father" he said with a wicked smile.

"I'll never come with you; I'll never go back there! You can go and tell them that!" I retorted; the man got taken aback.

Then he frowned, grabbed my arms and tied them behind my back. I didn't dare try and fight. I saw that a gun was tucked in his belt. Another person held Tai's hands behind her back. She looked at me determinedly. She used eye movements to gesture the nearby clearing where our captors were taking us. There were four others, luckily, weren't armed, as far as I could notice.

I nodded and I swept my foot across the floor in an arc then kicked my captor square in the chest. He dropped the weapon and went flying. Then Tai did the same when her captor was distracted.

Two of the people came at me and one of them fell forward with a suppressed thud, revealing Tai behind him. I then whisked around and threw a reverse kick at the other one.

I saw two people jump from the trees, it was the boys, Marat and Jian landed on two of the men. Kai landed behind me, knelt and started fumbling with the ropes that bound my hand.

The ropes hit the leaf-covered ground with a muffled thud, "Thanks"

"You're welcome!" he replied.

There was an indistinct click of a pistol; I had forgotten to pin down the man who had tied me up.

He fired, I tried to dodge it, but it stroked my shoulder. I recoiled and gasped.

Other clicks aimed at Tai; the bullets whistled over her head as she threw herself to the side fell into a crouch.

There was a dull thud; Jian had catapulted a heavy stone at the man!

Chapter 13

The French Concession

We all backed away from the scene and followed Marat, who had the compass, in the south-westerly direction. We arrived at a civilization, but we were in heavily occupied Japanese territory. Tai gestured for us to come. She led us to a battered lorry which was heading towards the market that was close to the concession. We climbed on its back unnoticed.

When the lorry arrived at its destination, we ran non-stop to the allocated house. Grandma Xu was waiting at the door for us and breathed a sigh of relief. She led to thin beds at the back of the house but all the same it was comfortable to be somewhere that was safe, for now.

I snapped up; the light was dim. There was a stiff bandage around my shoulder down to the upper arm, restricting my movement.

"Relax, I think you have had quite an adventure", it was my mother's voice. She pushed me back down on my stretcher.

"The soldiers are most likely recovering from the beating they got from the boys," she explained, motioning towards the four other figures on similar beds who were next to me.

Marat, who was sitting upright smiled at me, "Looks like we have really had an adventure" he chuckled. He cast a sideways glance at his sister, next to him.

"Thanks for being tolerant of her. She really appreciates it"

"Don't worry, I kind of had the same experience too" I replied.

"It must have been difficult for you," he said.

He did not mean it; I knew that he didn't. There was a pause. "If you don't me asking, how do you understand Tai so well?" I asked.

"Well, you see, we've grown up with each other for so long I grew to understand her. I could say we're part of the same person, one mind but two bodies"

"Things got difficult over the years, especially when my mother passed away in Thailand and my father died in Tibet. We were lost in our own minds, didn't know what to do, but Grandma Xu let us stay with Kai in the Academy. Japanese patrol got worse after 3 years or so."

"That must be an extremely hard time to get through... But I've got to admit that being able to understand her without speech is helpful"

He smiled weakly and then said "It's helpful, but it's got a disadvantage too"

I was surprised, "How can it be a disadvantage?"

"One day we were going to Changxing Island, you know the Island West of Hengsha, to give a code to an agent. Someone had betrayed us and Japanese were waiting. We tried to fight them. Tai had put the paper, bearing the code under a brick in the alleyway, but they took her away..." he trailed off.

"That must have been hard for both of you!"

"That was the disadvantage, especially for me. It was first time I had been separated from her, it felt as if I was torn in half"

I knew it really could have felt like that by the sound of his tone.

I wanted to change the subject, so I asked what they did with the soldiers.

"They kept us busy for a while, but we knocked them out eventually. Then we used their own rope and tied them to bamboo clusters. It took us some time to track you too."

"I wonder what's happened to them" I said thoughtfully.

Grandma Xu came in and sat down next to me, "All of you have done extremely well, especially with the Japanese soldiers. You managed to buy us time to escape. I'm sorry that this happened to you Lei. We were all worried because you children were taking so long but at least you were all in one piece. I am so proud of you all"

"it's-"

"I know, the important thing is to get rest. You have school in a few days. So, now it's time to recover" and she gently pushed me back down onto my stretcher again.

"One last question?" I asked her.

"Ok, just one".

"Why aren't we in a hospital?"

"The Japanese will easily find you in a public hospital and besides, the Concession is safer. They will have to ask for permission to enter so that means we would have time to escape. Lei, you have done well, far more than many can imagine. I advise you to get some rest" she said gently.

The next two days we stayed at the Concession, at my mother's friend's house. They weren't the best of friends, but the lady was willing to help the resistance.

The place reminded me of my father's house on the outside. The tarmac roads, concrete walls, little greenery. On the inside the house was kept clean and tidy, but it had warmer colours on the inside. The woman was kind but a little fussy of how and where her ornaments were kept. I have to say that it is remarkable how she remembers when something had been touched.

I saw a tiny violin sculpture about the size of my thumb. I picked it up and was examining the intricate details of it, then I put it down exactly as it was. At dinner that day she said that anyone touching ornament should be careful. I was so shocked that she realized it. All the same she tried to make us as comfortable as possible.

My mother explained that she didn't know this woman very well. It's just that Zhou Fen told me about her. "So, she's basically my friend's friend." On our last day there, the woman warned us about the search for me was widening.

Chapter 14

Topaz

A week passed and we had returned to Hengsha Island. I still wasn't allowed to take off my bandages. I couldn't help just realizing that my mother seemed to be spending less time with me now even though she could now walk. I wasn't sure why.

The last day of the week was about to end and my mother came back home with a huge box in her hands, her smile was full of pride.

"What is it Mama?"

"Just wait and see" she said, she walked slowly and carefully towards my room.

"Shouldn't Grandma Xu see too?"

"She already knows Lei" she chuckled.

"Can't we open it in the kitchen?"

"I think this is the best place to open it because then your room should be the first room for it to see. Now be quiet when I opened this". I was so confused by my mother's behaviour.

She opened the box and I saw a bamboo cage. It had beautiful carvings on it. She took something else out of the cage; it was another box, lined with linen cloth, it also had small holes. She opened the small box and I saw a tiny bundle of colourful feathers and pair of tiny eyes full of curiosity, "It's a chick!". I exclaimed.

My mother smiled, "It's a turquoise parakeet chick" she said.

"She's beautiful!" I gasped. I gently scooped the tiny budgie chick in my hands. It started trying to jump off my hand although she couldn't fly. I cupped it in my hands and gently put in on my bed.

"Beautiful, isn't she?" said my mother.

"Yes, she is. Is she for me?"

"Yes, she is a gift for your bravery!"

"Thank you, Mama"

"I also got her for free"

"How? Aren't these birds quite expensive"

"Well, she was the weak one of the litters and so the shop owner was thinking of throwing her with the rubbish"

"How could they do such a thing to a helpless creature?"

"It is cruel isn't it? They think it will ruin their reputation, you see. If I had come a day later then I would have got a totally different bird!"

"I will look after her as well as I can"

"First, you need to name her, don't you?".

I looked around my room and saw the amber Topaz ring on my mother's finger. Then I looked at the chick's crest. The colours matched.

"Her crest is the colour of the amber Topaz, on your ring Mama. I'll name her Topaz"

"Beautiful name" she said. "And remember she will need soft, quick hands and crucial support if she is to survive" warned my mother.

I had a good hour with Topaz; I let her down on the floor and I saw she was weak because she kept falling over and I kept helping her up. (Topaz pooped a couple of times on the floor, but it was tiny). Soon she got used to me helping her walk. The thing I loved most of all is that Topaz seemed to understand me that I was helping her.

I was surprised she didn't try to run away when I held her by hand to feed her. I scooped some of her feed with my other hand and moved it close to her so she could reach. She tried to eat the seeds, but she couldn't swallow them yet. So, I gently put her down on my desk, got a pencil and crushed the seeds into smaller pieces with the end of it. I pushed the crushed seeds closer to Topaz and she ate her food happily.

I left her in her cage (with a small tissue on the bottom in case she poops) and plenty of crushed seeds. "I won't be long Topaz, just going to get my friends. You be careful!" I whispered.

I ran down to the beach were the Jian and Kai were messing around in the sea and Marat was sitting on the sand sketching something, "Boys! Come and see, I've got something to show you!" I half shouted, happily.

"What is it?" asked Kai.

"Just come out of the sea and I'll show you!"

"Ok, we are coming!" chuckled Jian.

I crossed my arms with my back to them and waited for them to come out, "What is it Lei?" asked Marat who came next to me. "You all follow me, and I'll show you!" I chuckled.

"Come on!" I said, as soon as they had dried themselves. I started sprinting as fast as I could towards the house.

I stopped in the garden and I turned around to see if the boys had come; Jian came first, but he stopped so abruptly that Kai crashed into him and Marat tripped over them. I burst out laughing and my mother opened the door and saw the tangle and she joined in laughing too.

Finally, four of us stood outside my bedroom door, "You have got to keep very quiet" I whispered.

"Why?" asked Marat, he forgot to talk quietly. I kicked him and put my finger to my lips and opened the door.

The cage was empty! I began searching frantically around my room and I found Topaz behind the cage. She was investigating the curtains. I drew in a breath of relief.

"Hey, what are you doing there?" I asked her as I scooped her up to show to the boys.

"Wow! She is so colourful! Who gave her to you?" asked Jian.

"My mother gifted her to me"

"Have you given her a name?"

"Yes, I have. Her name is Topaz"

"Wow! Suits her well. Can we hold her too?"

"Yes, you can", I gently let her down on Jian's bandaged hand, Topaz gently chewed the end of the bandage curiously. "She is so light" asked Jian, looking closely at her.

"She is the runt of the litter and she was quite weak. So the shop owner was about to throw her away when my mother came",

"Do they really do this to creatures like her?"

"Yes, because they think it will ruin their reputation"

"Let's take our mind off that and play with Topaz" suggested Marat.

"Good idea" agreed Kai.

We put her on the floor and sat down to help her walk. She ate a lot more food than I had expected. "She is growing so she will need quite a bit of food to grow especially when they are below average" explained Marat. "She will need crucial support if she is to survive" My mother had warned me.

Topaz was able to walk and climb up my bed sheets and curtains without support in the next few weeks because her talons had grown well. She could also carry some small keys in her beak when she was strong enough. I went to bed after playing with Topaz and put her in her cage with the lock on.

I climbed on my bed and got out a book to read and suddenly she was on my pillow,

"How did you get out of the cage Topaz? I don't know how but you have got stay in your cage to sleep" and I scooped her up and placed her inside the cage and locked it. Then I saw something extraordinary; She opened the lock with her beak and climbed on my hand. "How did you learn to do that?" I whispered, "But you have got to stay in your cage" and I put my hand in for her to climb off, but she didn't. "|So, you don't want to go in your cage?".

I brought her to my bed and sat down. I got my book out and Topaz climbed on the book as I started to read. After a while I got sleepy. So, I got an extra pillow from under my bed and put it on the foot-end of the bed and placed Topaz on it.

Chapter 15

Chongqing

It was late-July and now Topaz could fly well and pick up small objects like a small leaf or a crumb of a biscuit.

There was a tense atmosphere around the adults that day. "Why do you look worried Mama?" I asked.

"Our agents tell us that American pilots are getting ready to bomb Japan on August 6 and we have to head to Chongqing tomorrow because that is where some agents will be intercepting Japanese military codes" explained my mother.

"We four are coming too right?"

"Yes, you are"

"Can I take Topaz? She won't be troublesome!" as my mother held Topaz in her hands.

"She is a well-trained little bird. But are you sure she won't be any trouble?" She wondered.

"No, she won't be a trouble Mama. We also don't need to take her cage because she prefers to sleep outside it"

"Ok, then you can take her"

"Thank you!" I tapped my shoulder twice and said, "Come on Topaz!". Topaz flew from my mother's palm to my shoulder.

I thought to tell the boys about the plan and I needed to pack. I tried to open the door to their room and found Tai blocking the doorway. When I opened, she turned around and gave a small wave then motioned to the room which was in the state of a 'battlefield'. Clothes, books, stationary and loose paper was scattered everywhere.

A head popped up from behind a pile of clothes, "Hi Lei, you know we are all going to Chongqing, right?" said Kai.

"Yes, I know, I was actually going to tell you"

"Ok. Well, we're all packing; we can help you pack once we're done" suggested Jian.

"To be honest, I think you're the ones who need help!" I said.

Marat stood up and looked around the room as if he had just noticed the state of it. I caught his eye and raised an eyebrow. He chuckled nervously and shrugged, "I don't think we're never going to get the hang of being neat". I smiled.

"Ok! Time's up you're done" I said and we all proceeded to the other room. "Your room is so neat! Unlike ours!"

"But didn't you say you had maids at your house?" asked Jian.

I did my best to imitate her proud tone and "Yes, but my stepmother told them that I needed to be independent while she gets them to do her make-up and things like that!"

"Ok, I get it" said Marat.

I searched around my room for things that I would need; my books, clothes, my pen and notebook, bird seed and a small piece of cloth (for Topaz) while Tai packed her own things.

"Done!" I said, happily. We sat down on the floor and played with Topaz for a while. When we were about to go to the paddy fields, my mother came in and sat down next to me.

"Don't worry, go" she said to them. "Lei will join you in five minutes."

When they went out of my bedroom door, she turned to me, "Your auntie told me what happened to you Lei". She was talking about what happened to me at my father's house.

I froze, "Sorry, I didn't tell you" I replied.

"It's ok, I know you were trying to get over it. I don't blame you" She smiled at me. "It was unfair that he kicked you out, but I don't think his heart was in it. He loves you, it's just that woman who is making him do it to you."

"You think so?"

"Yes, I do. Your father might now not like that woman as much now, but he finds it hard to tell people to leave. But we have got something incredibly important to do. You can't be seen in Shanghai because the police are still looking for you by the looks of it"

"But auntie sent him a letter that we were living on Hengsha Island. Why is he still looking for me?"

"I don't know, but I don't think it is your father that is doing it. I think it is your stepmother that keeps doing it in your father's name"

"If that's the case Mama, I think the day when we rescued the prisoners from Bridge House, people that tried to kidnap me. And probably were sent by my stepmother? To demand more money from my father?" I wondered.

She looked surprised, "Really? She is some problem, but what you must understand is that there will always be people like that. It's you that should not let them interfere with your life". She hugged me and whispered, "Everything is going to be alright Lei".

It was July 31st we were preparing for a journey that will mostly be taken on foot for the next day. It was a busy day packing food, walking boots and other necessities for a travel that was around 891miles. That evening we ate dinner at 6:00pm and slept at 7:00pm for an early waking at 4:00am.

Someone was shaking me. There barely any light in my room. I opened my eyes a millimetre apart. Tai pointed to the clock to show that she had woken me up half an hour early.

"Th... thank you Tai" I yawned. Then Topaz' face popped upside down a few centimetres away from my face. I let out a short scream when Tai started laughing. Then I joined in. To be honest, it was very strange seeing someone laughing but hearing no sound.

An hour later, at 4:30pm we were riding on a meat delivery truck driven by an agent. My mother had told me to keep my hair covering my face slightly because they were still looking for me.

We got off at Hangzhou and thanked the driver. Grandma Xu held out a map, "It is best we go in more forest areas to avoid Japanese patrol.

The walk was long and tiring. We had reached a plateau of mountains and valleys. It was beautiful place, but we couldn't stop and enjoy it. We were all sweaty, exhausted and soon ran out of water. Night had fallen and we were still on the move. We were saving our food because if we ate, we would become thirstier.

"Grandma Xu! I hear a river!" shouted Jian. This had me snap out of my stupor.

The four of us rushed ahead and we found a river, cascading down a small waterfall!

"Let's fill our flasks" said Grandma Xu.

"You know what, this looks like a good place to stay for the night Grandma Xu" suggested my mother.

"Mm, that is true Taia, this does look like a good place" she inspected the place and finally agreed. We had brought three tents for me and Tai, my mother and Grandma Xu and one for Kai, Marat and Jian.

We had built bamboo platforms to raise the tents off the ground. They roughly had 1 foot of ground clearance.

"Why do we need such high platforms Grandma Xu? I asked.

"You never know when the monsoon strikes!" she replied.

After we had finished setting up our camp I sat down, got my pen and notebook and started adding to my story.

"Lei, come here" beckoned Marat.

"What?"

"Come here first"

"Um, ok", I crouched down next to them, "Why did you call me?"

"Because it is Kai's birthday in a little less than two weeks, on August 12th, we are trying to think of a present for him.

"Well, what does he like?" Jian thought hard, "He likes reading books, painting, he loves animals and his geographical skills are really good even though he doesn't like writing coordinates in class" said Jian

"Why don't we buy him a bird, like Topaz?" Marat suggested. She was sitting on my shoulder, nestled in my hair.

"Good idea, we can ask Grandma Xu, or Taia?"

"I'll ask my mother. She knows where these to get the best birds"

We had slept briefly but well. Our bodies deserved some rest after the long trek to this mountainous region. Just as Grandma Xu had predicted, the monsoon rains had started after we had lit our fire so Grandma Xu had built a roof of fresh, green leaves and bamboo poles, over the fire so the rain wouldn't extinguish it and the fire wouldn't burn the leaves. It was pouring for what seemed like forever I even wondered how the clouds could hold so much water.

No sooner we woke up than we were now in another truck heading towards Chongqing. We had got on near the Wu river, in Tongren.

At last, we were in Chongqing. It was way much more greenery than Shanghai. Almost like Hengsha except multiplied immensely. Little roads wove through ravines, over mountains, under sheer cliffs. The evening air smelled sweet to me, a girl who has grown up in a polluted city.

The place we were staying was enough for two weeks; a simple house barely furnished with two bedrooms (one en-suite), there one kitchen a living/dining room and a main bathroom. The house didn't have any windows; just bamboo frames where glass was supposed to be.

We five had one room, while the adults had the other. We took our hammocks that Grandma Xu had bought on the way and we tied them to the roof beams I had laid down my bag, with Topaz on it and just dropped myself in the hammock.

Morning of August 3rd, we were going to be taken to the hospital to check our wounds. Our wounds hadn't seen bandages or treated by professional doctors.

We travelled by rickshaw. When we approached the hospital, we saw that it had been built around a few trees because we saw the top of them sticking out of the building. It was, again, like Hengsha Island. The doctors were kind. I was accompanied by my mother for the treatment.

"Your cut is not shallow but not deep" said a doctor as she examined my shoulder.

"She won't need to stay in hospital any longer, will she?" asked my mother

"No, it will heal over time if I put a fresh bandage. Then if you come again next month, I'll check it. When it has healed your arm will be a little stiff"

"Ok" I said.

"So that means Lei won't need to stay in hospital" she replied, "I'll be see you next month. Thank you, doctor," said my mother as she led me out of the consultation room.

"You're welcome! And have a good day!" the doctor replied cheerfully.

"You too!"

We met the rest of the group in the waiting rooms. "How did your appointment go?" asked Grandma Xu.

"Good, I don't need to stay at the hospital. You?" I replied.

"We were good too, but they replaced my bandages and said it hasn't healed fully" said Jian, showing his wrist in a cast"

"Come, we have got to go to our house then to the landing place" urged Grandma Xu.

Chapter 16

Bombing of Hiroshima and Nagasaki

We arrived at our small house in Chongqing and a few minutes later there was a knock on the door. We all froze. Grandma Xu opened the door by a millimetre and peered round. She let a sigh of relief! It was Master Xu. He urged "Come, we need to go to meet our agents at the Yangtze river".

"Ok, let's go" agreed Grandma Xu.

We travelled in a horse-drawn cart to the small, square-roofed house with the tiles sloping upwards at the edges. There was a man and a woman waiting in the living room. I recognized them as Zhen and Tu, the twins we rescued from Bridge House. They both looked relieved to see us come, "Finally, you're here!" whispered Zhen.

"We just had these transmitters given to us by the valley" she said to Grandma Xu, who seemed to understand.

"Sit down, all of you, we have got long days ahead of us" insisted my mother and we were still soon to figure out that my mother really meant long days.

Tu put his hand on his friend's shoulder, "Taia, how are you? I see you are out of your wheelchair" he said.

"Yes, I'm fine, the journey has gotten me working again" she replied.

"Good, it's nice to see you are all well. You children are ok?" asked Tu, turning to us.

"Yes, we're fine, Jian still needs to recover though" I said motioning towards him.

"We're indebted to your bravery".

"It's ok" he replied.

"Jian, do you want to come with me? I can get some ointment.

The two days passed with the agents staying at the house for short periods of time going to receive or pass on codes and messages.

It was intense.

Grandma Xu woke us up at 2:00am in the morning on August 5th. Today was the day the bombs were to be released over Hiroshima, with Kokura and Nagasaki as alternative targets.

I was drifting in and out of my sleep after I had woken up. I slowly began to come out of my sleep and got up to sit next to my mother. "Mama, do they have to do this, do they have to bomb Japan?"

"No, they don't, they could just end the war here and bring peace to world for once. Yet, they remain mentally blocked, each side suspecting to be backstabbed after they surrender their weapons which will again precipitate another war"

"We are all humans. We all share this world. Why can't they understand? The war can only go so long"

"It is all filled with superstition and jealousy, the cause of this war. One day people will realize Lei, when this era is over"

"Ok"

Four hours passed and our ears were glued to the transmitters we had been given, trying to interfere any messages sent by the Japanese navy.

"Grandma Xu, a Japanese navy boat just reported 'Allied' aircraft flying approximately 176 nautical miles from Taiwan!

"Quick! We must inform the pilots quickly before they get shot down!"

I passed the transmitter to my mother, she radioed the pilot, Paul Tibbets who was flying the Enola Gay bombing aircraft.

"I would increase the altitude if I were one of the pilots" I suggested, "I don't want the Americans to be shot down, but I don't want to destroy the Japanese navy either."

"Good decision, Lei. The Co-pilot agrees with you" said Zhen.

"They are increasing their altitude, hopefully they will be shielded by the clouds" informed Jian.

An hour and a half passed, "Grandma Xu, the pilots are getting ready to bomb Hiroshima. They made to mainland unnoticed!" said Marat.

It was now 8:14am precisely, Tokyo time. I was listening intently to my transmitter; I heard the voices of the Navigator, Captain Theodore and the Bombardier, Major Thomas Ferebee. They were assembling to drop the bomb, Little Boy.

8:15am struck, the bomb was released, "They've done it, they've bombed Hiroshima" I said in an audible whisper.

I thought of how much lives have been lost at that very moment. Children playing in their gardens, newlywed couples, some were even taking their first ever breath, yet they were all going to take their last. It seemed merciless. Just because of one man's belief and greed, so many lives had to be lost.

There was news the next day. The scheduled bombing of Kokura was to be moved forward two days instead of August 11th due to bad weather.

I was outside when Tai came and sat down next to me, "seems unfair doesn't it?" I said, staring out into the distance.

She nodded.

"Yes, it does...but that's just how it is" said Marat.

"Where is Topaz?" asked Jian, breaking the silence.

"She's gone out for a fly; she knows how to find her way back"

"Really? You've taught her that too? That's amazing!" said Jian.

"Thank you"

And barely after I had finished my sentence, Tai pointed at the darkening sky and moments later I saw the outline of Topaz.

I stood up and held out my hand for her to land on.

That evening my aunt arrived at the house.

The morning of August 9th, again we woke early but at 3:00am, I was still drifting in and out of sleep.

3:40am, the Americans were getting ready to take off. The aircraft carrying the bomb was Bockscar piloted by Major Charles W. Sweeney and Captain Charles Donald Albury. The Enola Gay was also setting off once more, except the pilots were by Captain George W. Marquardt and Second Lieutenant James M. Anderson. The Great Artiste was also joining the bombing raid.

"The B-29s have taken off, precisely at 3:49am" informed Kai.

It was now late afternoon, "Grandma Xu, The Great Artiste has assembled at rendezvous but another aircraft that was supposed to meet at is not on the scene and General Charles Sweeney insisted to wait longer!" I said.

"But that will increase fuel consumption!" said Kai

"I'll radio Bockscar" said Grandma Xu and after she spoke with the General, "I don't know what the General is trying to do, but he says he's got enough fuel to wait longer" she said.

Tai tapped my shoulder and motioned to her transmitter. Grandma Xu looked questioningly at us. "The Enola Gay has just reported that Kokura and Nagasaki are within the parameters for the required visual attack" I reported what I had just heard from Tai's transmitter.

"Ok, Zhen, Kokura is the primary target, isn't it?" asked my Auntie.

"Yes, if there is a problem bombing Kokura then they will most likely redirect to Nagasaki"

"Ok" She replied.

"The General has just left the rendezvous point over Yakushima Island. He is heading to Kokura accompanied by The Great Artiste" said my mother.

Half an hour later Bockscar reported clouds and drifting smoke. "Grandma Xu, they're saying that delays at the rendezvous point has resulted in the smoke coming from Yahata, the nearby town bombed by 224 B-29s yesterday. The crew of The Great Artiste says that almost 70% of Kokura is covered with smoke" reported Marat.

"So how will they get a visual of Kokura?" I asked.

"The General intends to try and do a bombing raid over Kokura despite these events" said Tu.

"But he has already burnt more fuel than expected!" said Jian.

45 minutes passed, "Grandma Xu, they are already trying their third bombing run!" said Marat "The bombardier cannot release the bomb visually!"

"But they are exposing themselves to Yahata's heavy defenses" I interrupted"

"What is he trying to do?" asked my mother.

Bockscar had completed its third bombing run. "General, divert to Nagasaki, further South so you will have enough fuel to land" said my mother, speaking through her transmitter.

She finished talking. "They have agreed to head South, down to Nagasaki then they will hopefully have enough fuel to head down to Iwo Jima"

We waited, listening to the regular reports from the Americans.

It was 10:57am precisely. They were assembling for the release of the bomb.

As the next minute struck, the bomb was released. 43 seconds later it exploded with a blast with an altitude of 1650ft (500m) high.

"The bomb exploded approximately 1.5 miles (2.4km) Northwest of the planned target. The Great Artiste has reported" my Auntie said.

"At least we have got the bombing out of the way as the airmen are critically low on fuel. They cannot make it to Iwo Jima, so they are planning to land on Okinawa Island, which is closer to Nagasaki"

"How does the control tower know?" asked Tu.

"We will have to try and contact the tower because the Americans are already 200 nautical miles from Okinawa. We just need to hope there aren't any patrol boats there"

We kept trying to reach the control tower, but the radio kept going static. If we could contact the Americans, then why couldn't we reach the tower? I thought.

"Jian, did they start the bombing raid from the pacific side?" I asked him.

"No, they were flying over the East China Sea" he replied.

I gasped, "Grandma Xu, I know why we can't contact the tower!" I blurted

"Why?" she responded.

"Because Okinawa Island is on the far side of the East China Sea and we don't have enough range!" I exclaimed.

There was silence.

"We're going to lose contact with the Americans, they will have to contact the tower when they get there" I said.

Everyone agreed.

We continued communicating with Bockscar for the rest of the journey. They were getting increasingly low on fuel each minute and the stakes were high. We were slowly losing contact with them.

Finally, they reached Okinawa after they had been circling for 20 minutes trying to contact the control tower. "General, your radio maybe faulty, there is no choice for you but for you to execute an emergency landing procedure. There is only enough fuel to do it once" My mother had warned the General. He managed to interpret the static and agreed.

"Auntie, tell them to fire flares to warn them of the unclear landing" I suggested.

"Good thinking Lei" she said, and my auntie informed the airmen to do so.

"They've started descent" said Zhen.

"What! They're going too fast to land, landing at 150 miles per hour!" exclaimed my mother.

"They have no choice Taia. They have no time to slow down otherwise they will run out of fuel" explained Zhen.

They had started descending and engine number two died from fuel starvation. It was a half-controlled landing. They touched the runway, hard, it took some time before the pilots regained control of the plane, but they were still speeding down the runway,

"Grandma Xu! They're going too fast, and they're going to fall off the runway!" attested Jian.

"The B-29s reversible propellers are insufficient to slow the aircraft adequately and the brakes are also not enough!" said Marat

"The only thing they can do is to turn away from the end of the runway, "but with that much speed I don't know if that is possible" said Grandma Xu.

"Grandma Xu, it's the only chance we've got to save their lives as we are forever in their debt" said my mother.

She radioed Bockscar, "the crew also agree" she said after she had talked to them.

"They're going to try it" she added.

We all waited; the atmosphere was intense. There was static on our transmitters, "This is...Bockscar, we...successfully landed", it was the General's voice.

We all breathed a sigh of relief! **The War was surely over**.

Chapter 17

Caves

A few days passed and I woke up in my bedroom in that little house on the island. I remembered something vitally important. I turned around shook Tai awake. Then we both crept into the boys' room and tiptoed towards Jian's bed seeing as it was the closest. He was sleeping on his front with his face buried in the crook of his elbow. Tai shook him gently and he just murmured in his sleep. She shook him harder; he still didn't wake up. So, I pushed him off his bed, and he jerked awake. "Ow! What was that for?" he said, half asleep.

"To wake you up!" I whispered. I shook him even harder, "Ok, ok! I'm up!", he looked at me and said, "why did you wake me up this early?"

"We've got something important to do, remember!"

"What? oh, yeah uh (as I whispered in his ear) ... Do we really have to do it this early?"

"Yes, otherwise Kai will notice it!" I retorted.

"Ok! Ok!"

"Wake up Marat and come to my mother's room"

"Ok..." he said sleepily

"And don't go back to sleep!" I warned.

"I won't!". Tai smiled and gave a silent nod.

We walked quietly, down the corridor to my mother's bedroom. The door was open. I found her brushing her hair in front of the silver-rimmed mirror. "Hello Lei! I got up early as you children asked!"

"Thank you, Mama! I hope it wasn't too much to ask"

"You can ask anything Lei! And it's no trouble. Even though I'm starting shifts at the veterinary surgery, I made it so I could spend time with you too!"

"Thank you!"

"It's nothing. Anyway, are those two boys up yet?"

"They should be" I said, looking over my shoulder towards the corridor", she laughed. "When your auntie, Master Xu and I were children, Master Xu always used to sleep lately until he was in college and once, he forgot to attend a lesson."

"Really? I thought he always used to wake up early! He looks like it"

"Now he does, before, you wouldn't even recognize him!"

We both laughed as she explained about how she and my auntie would wake him up suddenly. Ten minutes later, Jian and Marat came in.

"Hello boys, so what's the plan?"

"Mm, well, we've planned to buy a reasonable sized bird for him, like Topaz" explained Marat.

"Oh, ok! That's no problem, I know about lots of different types of birds that I have looked after in my days" my mother chipped in.

"So, do you have any pictures of these birds?" asked Jian.

"Yes! Loads of them, in fact I have a picture of almost every bird I have treated!"

"Can you show us all of them?" asked Marat.

"Sure!" She replied

My mother showed us all the bird species she had looked after. "Look at these photos, I've arranged the species in files. Here is the Conures... Cockatiel and Cockatoo... Amazons... Kakariki... Eastern Rosella... Blue-headed Parrot... the Electus... Budgies... and the Macaws", we had been through all the files that my mother had got.

"Which one gets along with Parakeets?" asked Marat.

"Why?" asked Jian.

"Because Kai can't have a bird that will attack Topaz" I said.

"Exactly" added my mother, with a smile. "The ones that get along well with parakeets are the amazons, the kakariki, Cockatiels, Cockatoos and budgies" she said.

"I quite like the red-fronted Kakariki" said Marat, looking through the labelled file.

"Same" I agreed.

"But how big are they?" asked Jian.

"They're only an inch or so bigger than the budgies" said my mother.

"Ok then! I say the Kakariki's too" agreed Jian.

"That's great! I've packed breakfast for you all and it's in the kitchen, don't forget to take your backpacks. Let's go, before Kai wakes up!"

"What if he does though"? I asked

"Then Grandma Xu will say you have all gone to revise at Sunday self-study sessions" my mother replied.

We had gotten into a small sampan and were heading towards South of Shanghai, to a place where my mother knew the best birds were sold.

The location was probably surrounded by so much forest that the rickshaw had to go off-road for a while. The building was not really a building. It was a bunch of trees with a few wood planks sealing the gaps between them. When we paid the driver of the rickshaw, he looked at the house uncertainly and left.

"This is one of my colleague's house. He has retired and prefers being far from the city noise" said my mother.

"Really far" added Marat.

"Mm.. hm" said Jian, nodding his head.

"Let's go inside" said my mother

"Are you sure this is a civilized house?" I asked.

"Sure, it is! I came here a few days ago. Wait until you get inside, it's so interesting||!"

Three of us exchanged glances and looked uncertainly at my mother and we walked toward the house without another word.

I knocked the door of the shack which was barely holding on to its hinges and it fell even with one knock. Luckily, Grandma Xu had trained our reflexes to avoid any sudden dangers that might occur. I had jumped back so fast that I hit Marat, who was admiring a fusion of two tree-trunks behind us. He was smashed into the tree.

"Ow!" he exclaimed

"Whoops, sorry!", I was struggling to keep my face straight while my mother, Jian and Tai were laughing so much that their eyes were filled with tears.

"I can't see! It's too blurry!" said Jian.

"Wait, here you go" said my mother. She got a small towel out of her bag and gave it to him.

"Thank you, Taia" he said

"You're welcome" she replied, "Now, let's see who's home". The three of us peeked round the door frame, there was one low-roofed room. Tucked in a corner sat a wooden box with a gone-off mango on it. Further in the shack was a wooden chair with a leg missing and behind that was a raised part of the floor with a bamboo frame with thick vines weaved in and out (I assumed that was a bed). On the floor was a very long ladder-like frame, which was probably a part of the roof that collapsed inwards.

"Uh, Taia, I don't think anyone lives here" said Jian.

"I thought that he wouldn't leave the house like this" she replied.

"Then why did we come here?" asked Marat.

"Because he lives here, below"

"Below?" I asked

"Let me show you", my mother crouched down and went inside. She walked towards the thing that I assumed was a bed and she examined it. She took a piece of paper out of her pocket and read something. She put the piece of paper back and chuckled, "He is a clever one". My mum turned to us and said "Come"

We three exchanged glances again and looked befuddled.

"Come, I'll show you" she said. She dug her fingers under the bamboo frame and tugged it...nothing happened. She pulled even harder... bang! It came free, revealing a roughly circular hole with water at the bottom. It was a well.

My mother took the frame that was laid on the floor and slid it down into the hole until it reached the bottom.

"Wait, are we going to climb into the well!?" said Marat

"Yes" my mother replied simply.

"Isn't that dangerous?" asked Jian.

"Just watch and see" she replied. Then she was about to climb into the hole when she said "Oh, yes, I suggest you take off your shoes and put them in your bags. You don't want them to get wet, do you?"

We looked uncertainly and took off our shoes.

"Good, now come when I say it's ok to climb down"

"Uh, ok" I said unsurely. My mother started climbing down, the hole was quite wide, but two people couldn't fit. The climb seemed deeper than I thought. I heard splashing at the bottom...silence there was not a sound, "Mama! Are you ok?" I asked.

"Yes, I am, just checking", her voice echoed up the tunnel. When I poked my head into the hole, I couldn't see her, there was just water. "Mama, where are you. I can't see you!"

"I know you can't" she replied, "Now Lei, come down!" she said

"Ok!", I looked at the Tai, Marat and Jian and they looked back, confidently. I climbed down, the walls were slimy and wet, I kept my elbows from touching it. The climb seemed like forever; the tunnel was uneven too. My feet finally touched water. But my mother wasn't here. I got so shocked when I heard her voice though; "Lei, the water is probably going to go up to your waist"

"Yes Mama, But where are you?" I asked.

"Past the tunnel", I looked around and saw a small semi-circle hole, just enough for me to crouch down and go.

Chapter 18

Underground base

The small hole lead to an opening. I climbed out and a huge cavern revealed itself and I saw my mother beside the opening, "That was a little adventure, wasn't it?" she said.

"Yes! It was!" I said, smiling. "Shall I call them down?"

"Ok", I went back down the tunnel "It's ok to come down!"

A minute later Jian popped out of the opening closely followed by Tai and Marat.

Tai looked at Marat pointedly as he said " Tai put the frame back on the bed, because she felt like it was necessary" said Marat

"Good, you children are also taking safety measures" my mother replied.

"Uh, Taia, where are we?" asked Jian

"This, Jian, is where my friend's house is" she said. We all looked at the huge cavern.

'Are we doing all this for one bird?' I thought.

"Follow me" said my mother. We all followed. She led between many slippery stalagmites and to a small cleft in the rock. There was a strange line in the rock though. My mother slapped the wet rock in a continuous pattern three times. The sounds echoed eerily against the limestone walls. The rock slid, slow but significant.

"Taia! So good to see you!" came a voice from behind the boulder.

"Chen, how did you manage the Japanese?"

"They're not troubling me much since I have moved here"

"I can see why!" my mother chuckled, the man looked at us and said, "Are these the children?"

"Yes, they are".

"Great! Come inside, you all look cold". He finally pushed the stone aside, revealing a strong figure. He looked around the age of fifty.

We stepped inside, instead of a cold, draughty house I had imagined, the house's floor was made from a polished stone and the walls were painted with cinnamon colour. The house was furnished well, and almost everywhere there were birds.

"Sit here, warm yourselves up" he said.

"Wow! You've really made yourself at home Chen!" said my mother.

"How did you do this?" I asked

"Well, you see, I used to work as a stonemason and so I carved out this house. And then I got help from my friend, who makes furniture and, that's my house. I also moved some of my old furniture here." he explained.

"Whoa, that must have taken a while" mentioned Jian.

"Well, it only took two weeks, add a few more days"

"I thought it would take at least a month, to carve out this stone as well" I remarked.

"I decided to make it quick, before the Japanese knew what I was doing. I concluded to work 16 hours a day"

"That must have been hard" my mother said.

"Why are the Japanese worrying you?" I asked.

"I am one of the main people who pass on messages and communicate hugely with the resistance. I was your contact from Shanghai during the recent bombs. Unfortunately, the Japanese found out, but my friends warned me quickly. Now I have made this an underground base for some meetings instead" he said, "Anyway, are you children ok? I heard what happened"

"Yes, we're fine, but how did you know?" I asked.

"How do I know? I'm Zhou Fen's father, she told me" he said.

"Thank you for rescuing Fen. How did you do it? The Kempeitei's defenses are almost impossible to penetrate?"

"It was a great teamwork!" I replied.

"Really?! Well done!", I flushed at this compliment.

"Thank you" I said.

"So, let's get to the reason why you came here, you wanted a red-fronted kakariki, right?" he said.

"Yes, we wanted it as a present for my brother" said Jian.

"Ok, do you want a chick?"

"If you have one, yes please" said Marat.

"Good, follow me", and he led us to another room with lots of bamboo cages. "Here are the chicks, and luckily you came at this time because I only have one Kakariki chick left"

"Where is he?" I asked.

"Hmm, just look at that pile of lemons" he replied.

"Uh, we came here for a bird, not a lemon" said Jian.

Chen chuckled, "Look closer" he said. I looked closer at the pile of lemons and saw a feathery heap that was lemon-yellow amongst the smooth lemons.

"I see it!" said Marat.

"Me too! Can we touch him?" I asked.

"Yes, but first you have to earn his trust" he explained. Then he scooped up the chick as he revealed his face. He had a small red marking on his head and soft, lemon yellow feathers. The chick looked at us with eyes full of curiosity.

"He's so beautiful! I love the red markings on his head!" whispered Jian.

Chen smiled and said, "I think it is safe for you to touch him. He isn't scared, which is a good start" he whispered,

"Who wants to go first?" When he said this, the three of them pointed at me. "Why me?" I asked.

"Because you know how to approach them-" said Marat.

"-and I just think you should go first" interrupted Jian.

Tai nodded in agreement.

"Ok, ok, I'll go first" I said. I approached the little bird and lifted a finger and placed it on his head. He felt so soft that I couldn't really feel him. After a while, when we had all touched him, he started nibbling the tip of my nail. "It tickles!" I said.

"You are more of a natural than I thought. You've bonded with him well" he said.

My mother had given a small scroll to Chen just before we left. The little bird was chirping excitedly in his bamboo cage.

"Mama, how are we going to get out? We surely can't go back up the well, especially when there is no ladder" I said.

"This cavern has lots of natural exits and entrances. The one we are going to leads to the North-easterly side of this mountain. We came in at the South-side of it. Now, follow me" she explained.

"Taia, what was in that scroll that you gave him? I had a feeling we didn't go there just for a bird" said Jian.

"Good question, you see, the prisoners are still in Shanghai and they need proper medical treatment for their wounds.

So, we need to transport them to Chongqing without being caught. The Japanese will bound to be checking the vehicles by now. And I gave Chen the coordinates of the place where the prisoners are." said my mother.

"But how can he help? The Japanese are looking for him too" said Marat.

"He did say that he was one of the people who pass on the messages and he might pass it on without going out of his home. I simply took the advantage of you children wanting a bird and so I put the two jobs on one string" she said.

That was a clever idea, I thought.

"Now, it should be somewhere here..." said my mother, muttering to herself. Then she took out a small chisel from her bag and started tapping the rock wall with it. The wall sounded strangely hollow.

"This looks like the place" said my mother, looking at her compass. She began to tap the hollow wall and it started to chip away slowly.

She had finally made a hole big enough for her to fit through, "Follow me" she said and disappeared into the hollow wall. I entered after her and saw a natural passageway where water would have flowed down. The floor was smooth but dry and it seemed that water hadn't flowed here for a while.

"...I told him to block this hole. So, in time it would be safe to climb through, once it's dry" my mother explained. Her voice was echoed strangely against the enclosed rock walls

"Taia, how do you know these caves so well? You've only been here once, right?" asked Marat.

"Well, I've been here countless times, as a child, with Master Xu and Jia Li. Look, this is the hole that we had carved when we were little, I can't believe I was this small!" she said.

"Can you fit through?" I asked.

"No, but I am going to chip away the edges, this might take a while because the rock is harder", as she said so I heard the steady chipping of the chisel on rock.

Around fifteen minutes later we had come out of the gap in the mountain. I noticed that we had come further inland. We walked for an hour when we arrived at a small town.

We had paid for a rickshaw to take us to the coast, where we had boarded a sampan.

Chapter 19

August 12th

It seemed that the afternoon was very bright now because we had been in the dark caves. The water of the Yangtze river was still and quiet.

I was at the bow of the sampan staring out into the distance, wondering what will happen next. What will happen after some of the major cities in Japan had been bombed. "Will they surrender?' or 'Will they attack us more ferociously?" Those were my two questions for the future.

"You ok?" asked Jian, from behind me. I jumped!

"You scared me Jian! And yes, I'm ok. Just wondering what's going to happen next"

"With the Japanese?"

"Yes"

"They're bound to surrender. They must. Otherwise, they will get bombed again! I think"

"I hope you're right"

"You know, I had the same feeling a long time ago"

"When?"

"It was 1941 and I was 9 years old at the time. That was a terrifying experience, if you ask me"

"What happened?" I asked.

"Well, as you know I was enrolled for the classes at the academy. My father had taken me to Tibet, near Zhari Namco, for coordinating a project with the resistance. It was something complicated and extremely dangerous. Meanwhile, my mother had gone to Siam (Thailand) to help over there. I didn't really understand what they were doing, but I knew it was important. I was left in my father's friend's house.

On the evening of December 8th my father had come back from a meeting. Moments later an agent from the meeting had come rushing home with worrying news. Japan and Siamese troops had been fighting for hours; Japan demanded a passage through the country for their forces, who had invaded Burma (Myanmar) to Malaysia. The Siamese troops had just yielded"

"Why did they make it so easy for Japanese to get through?"

"It's just like you said, they probably didn't want war to affect their country, so they had no choice but to surrender"

"I guess so" I agreed, I was really shocked, 'They gave up so soon?' I had thought.

"My mother was meant to come back the next day. But then she was trapped in Siam. We never heard from her.

My father sent me back to Shanghai as soon as possible. He said he will come back as soon as possible, but he never did" Jian continued.

I thought about it and said cautiously, "Did you ever find out why?"

"No, but two years later, Grandma Xu thought I was old enough to understand the most horrible reason why my father didn't return. Someone had betrayed the resistance on the same night just an hour before the Siamese had surrendered. My Father had to come back from the meeting to send me home quickly."

"Who was it? Do you know?" I asked, desperately.

"No, we've never seen his face. His last position was in Sichuan Province, in Chengdu. Grandma Xu only knows him by the code 9702." he admitted.

"Why would this '9702' person want to betray us?" I asked.

"Well, you saw those fishermen at Hengsha. You've seen how poor they are. No one would blame them for accepting money" he explained.

"You're suggesting that they bribed this agent?" I wondered.

"Yes, I think so. Also, Grandma Xu thinks that because these agents are trusted, 9702 probably told the Siamese agents that there was a bigger plan and so if they surrendered then they could trap the Japanese. Or at least something like that"

"Even a child wouldn't do that, that suggestion is highly illogical! -" I protested.

"- I know, I know! But this is what we guessed and we may not know the entire story. Agent 9702 just somehow convinced them to surrender" he added, briefly.

I stared out, looking at the shape of Hengsha slowly crawling towards us.

"Do remember the 'Doolittle Raid'" he asked, changing the subject.

"Yes, I do, it was the first air operation to strike the Japanese archipelago, am I right? I replied.

"mm hmm, but it was a major blow when the fifteen aircrafts reached China after bombing Japan but crashed. I can't believe that one landed in Siberia!"

"Me neither. But three of the eight airmen who were captured were executed, leaving four complete crews out of five. Eventually, only 69 out of 80 returned to America"

"Jimmy Doolittle is the best airmen I have ever seen! He even landed a plane at 296 miles per hour!"

"What?!" I said, hardly believing my ears.

"Yes, he did".

"Talking about the Doolittle raid?" asked Marat from behind us, "I love the flying records he has achieved; altitude, speed..."

The sampan slowly drew closer to the worn-down jetty by the shore of Hengsha. We got off the boat, took our luggage and gave our thanks to the fisherman.

We all walked home, soaking wet and muddy but we were extremely excited to bring home the new chick.

We opened the door to our house and crept inside slowly.

Grandma Xu was in the kitchen, "Hello, have you got his present?" she asked.

"Yes, we have. Where is Kai?" I replied.

"He has gone down to the beach"

"Good, that will buy us time to change" added Jian. Our clothes were soaking and filthy.

Just as we were making our way to the corridor, the front door opened. We froze in our tracks.

"What is going on?", Kai's voice came from behind the door. He looked at us and crossed his arms. "You had a very adventurous self-study session?" he queried, raising an eyebrow. Marat chuckled nervously and gave a sheepish smile.

"We uh, we … fell into a lake" Jian added.

"You totally did. Then why are you wearing trekking clothes?" he asked.

I elbowed Tai, "Shall we just tell him the truth? I mean, we can't hide it forever" I whispered.

She gave a subtle nod.

"Well, we went to Shanghai, took a rickshaw through a bamboo forest entered a shack, we climbed down a well, entered a cavern, walked for half a kilometre underground, entered an underground base, broke a hollow rock wall, climbed through an ancient, natural aqueduct, reappeared on the South Shanghai and, well... we came here" I admitted.

Kai looked at us simply and said "Why?". Before I could answer a tiny chirp came from the cage covered with a towel, "Is that a bird?" he asked, "I thought I heard one".

I exchanged glances with my mother, she shrugged.

"Yes, it is" I said

"Really?"

"Yes, we bought it for you"

"Thank you so much!"

"You're welcome"

We all washed and got changed. I came to the boys' bedroom and saw the three of them sitting on the floor talking quietly.

"Come sit down Lei!" said Marat. I sat down next to him,

"what are you talking about?" I asked.

Marat had just opened his mouth "We-"

"-what bird you get me?" Kai interrupted suddenly.

"You're going to find out" I replied simply.

He sighed, "I thought you would tell me if I surprised you" he said.

"My friends have tried that on me many times, doesn't work" I replied with a shrug.

Then I noticed Jian hadn't said anything. When I saw his expression, I was a little confused, "Jian, why do you look, uh...constipated?" I asked.

Marat burst out laughing Jian's expression fell away and he started laughing too, "nice vocabulary!" Kai commented.

"But he did look constipated!" I said, "Why?"

"Because...because he is not very good at keeping secrets like these. So he is trying not to let out the type of bird we've bought Kai"

"Oh, ok" I chuckled.

Then the door opened to reveal Tai holding the bamboo cage with the cloth still covering it. My Mother followed her.

"What were you laughing about? I heard it all the way from the kitchen!" asked my Mother.

"I made a statement, but it sounded more like a joke" I explained.

"Ok, now sit down, Lei, go and close the door", I did as I was told and sat down.

She lifted the cloth and flurry of chirping followed.

"you got me something that looks like a red-fronted Kakariki, but it doesn't look one" Kai commented

"He is a Kakariki" said my mother.

"But he hasn't got a single green mark on him"

"He is pure yellow one, not common. I've only seen one before this chick my days. I thought you would like to have a one-of-a-kind bird"

"Really? Thank you!" he said excitedly.

"You're welcome" She replied.

We played with the chick, who Kai named 'Lemon' because of his lemon-yellow plumage.

It was August 14th and we four had woken up early to go to the beach. There was no one there and it felt like it was our beach at that moment. The breeze that ruffled our hair felt crisper than ever. The silence only broken by Topaz and Lemon's chirps and the faint scratch of Marat's pencil. It gave me a chance for my mind to wander off into the distance.

I had introduced Topaz to Lemon, for them to get along and for Topaz to teach Lemon how to fly. Topaz glided clean and fast. I could say Topaz was a bit of a show-off, but Lemon took it in well. I must admit that he learned to fly faster than I thought. And when he did, he followed Topaz everywhere, like she was his older sister. All I can say is that they soon became good friends.

Then suddenly an excited shout came from behind us, "Come, the four of you come! There is something you've got to hear!", it was my mother.

My head snapped around," Come on, let's go!", and I jumped to my feet and ran. Topaz was surprised and she started flying after me as fast as she could.

I approached our house as the door was open, but I couldn't stop at the speed I was at. I burst into the house and slowed down immensely but I still bumped into the rear wall.

"Slow down, take it easy!" said Grandma Xu.

I smiled and gave a shrug in reply.

A few moments later I heard a playful argument which contained familiar voices. The next thing I knew is that Jian and Marat were stuck in the front doorway (I assumed they were having a competition of who got in the house first). A mop of black-brown hair came out from behind the two of them and suddenly they popped out of the doorway and onto the floor. "That did the job!" said Kai

"Ok, come on, keep listening to the radio" said my mother.

We were listening intently, even Topaz and Lemon were quiet.

There was a speech in a language I couldn't recognize. It was also overlapped with static. There was a long static pause between the change of the radio.

My mother looked up and said "It is spoken in Korean. Korea is most likely going to be divided into two separate countries."

Then the radio started again.

My mother and Grandma Xu looked at each other.

"Jian, tell us what they are saying" said Grandma Xu.

"It's in Thai, th-they are saying that Japan has...unofficially... **s-surrendered the war**..." he trailed off with a tense whisper.

Then everything seemed to go in slow motion. Kai and Marat jumped up and cheered while my mother and Grandma Xu exchanged glances with each other. I looked at Jian and Tai with surprise.

I could see a dawn to the night; we had surely won.

Chapter 20

The beginning

The war had stopped that very same year on September 2nd, 1945, which was Japan's 'official' surrender.

It was the beginning of a new era.

My auntie and Master Xu got married in 1946. Later that year, Kai had got high grades in his high school subjects. In 1948 Tai, Marat and Jian had got their exam results with good grades too. The following year, I had gotten above 95% in my subjects.

Jian had taken a gap year once he secured his place in his university. By that time Kai had gone to university and was taking a veterinary degree, I joined university with Jian. I decided to study civil engineering, while Marat took a medical degree, Jian studied computer science and Tai studied physics.

By the time I had come out of university in 1955, I was 21 years old. Kai had come out of university two years before me and Marat had come the year after me. They had decided to stay in that same little house on the island and keep it until the future unfolded itself.

Marat had come one year after, and when he came, it felt like a lifetime since we had all seen each other. In 1957, that following year, I published my improved childhood stories and began writing new ones. Topaz and Lemon were having good times with Grandma Xu.

I had a job to design new, modern developments for China. Marat had work in the local hospital as a Paediatrician, Kai was working with animals, understanding how and what their behaviours were and Jian worked for a project that designed quicker, better computers.

My auntie and uncle inherited Grandma Liang's house because she passed away a few years before. As she had no children, in her will, she wrote that her house was to go to my auntie. Close to my aunt's house there was another house that belonged to Grandma Liang, so my auntie gave it to Grandma Xu and my mother.

That same year, in 1958, Kai had moved out of our house to live with his wife, Yazhu Tan who was a surgeon and worked at the same base as him. She was an artist and she happily agreed to illustrate the covers of my books.

I had just come home from a business trip to Tianjin. I had just unpacked and went to sit down. Marat had got time off work to pick me up from Longhua Airport in Shanghai and his shift had started again. So, he had to go giving me some peace. But I was so excited to see Topaz and Lemon again. Both of them were equally excited too and jumped onto each shoulder.

While I was sitting down on the sofa, my mother came in, "Lei, it's so nice to see you again!" she said excitedly. "Hello Mama! It's great to see you too!" I jumped out of the sofa and hugged her. "How are you? How is Auntie and uncle, and Grandma Xu?" I asked cheerfully.

"They are all well, Grandma Xu has slowed down but she is healthy. How was the trip? How was the new airplane ride? Interesting?" she asked happily.

"Yes, it was. The plane ride was awesome! I've never seen an aircraft designed for so many people! And there we saw the newest buildings my team had planned; they are amazing to see in a physical form! But it's very busy, I would rather be here" I gleefully said.

My mother put her arms around me and held me close to her. "I am happy that you enjoyed." she said, "I remember when you were 12 and wanted to see the world for yourself, and here you are now, doing it. Eleven years has already passed from that very moment.

She paused and looked at me, "I wanted to discuss something with you"

"Mm hmm"

"You've grown up and settled with your friends, you four considered yourselves as family when you met them. Now your own family is going to come, isn't it?"

"Yeah, I guess..."

"So, what are you going to do?"

"I'll see"

After a few months, as I assumed, my mother and auntie had found someone who worked in Shanghai as a civil engineer too. He used to be a student a Xian Xu academy. So, my mother knew him too. My mother, auntie, uncle and I went to his house. His name was Li Jie. He was good-tempered and kind, but he was more of a mathematician than an author. But he told me that he had already got my books last year and he loved them.

After we had left, and the marriage was to go ahead, now I was thinking of the upcoming stage in my life. I thought of my mother's marriage photo, in my bedroom, in my father's house. 'My father's house' I thought, and that was the first time in 11 years that I longed to visit my childhood home.

I thought of the few reasons why we didn't visit my father for a long time. The Japanese were looking for us when we had helped the prisoners of Bridge House escape. After the war, my mother and I had sent countless letters to my father, asking if he was ok, but alas no reply. We had decided to forget about it and assumed my stepmother was stopping our letters from reaching my father.

"Mama, before the next stage of my life starts, I want father to come". She did look shocked.
But she understood my eagerness and agreed to go looking for him.

We walked to my childhood home in that busy little street, the concrete buildings and tarmac roads, the same sign at the end of the road but when we turned the corner it was a completely different street to the one, I had last seen. The newest buildings had been built and some of them I had designed.

I walked slowly with my mother by my side. She was looking around the place in an expression of wonder. The front of my father's house was the same, the blue-grey door with a panel of translucent glass by the side of it, the little brass, shell-shaped knocker on the door I had always had a pleasure to knock it when I was a little girl. It felt as though I had travelled back in time as if I were coming back from school. There was a moment when I asked myself if this was real, if I was still the ordinary 12-year-old girl.

I touched the cold, brass knocker. I felt the spiral bit of the shell, as I had always done. I knocked the door. Moments later there was fussing inside, and the door opened. Unexpectedly, the maid opened the door. I remembered the smell of her food cooking in the kitchen, the times when she took me to the market. It was nice to see her again.

"Hello there, who are you here for?", she said kindly, with a smile. She couldn't recognise me.

"We are looking for Xian Zhao" I said.

"Ok. Well, come inside, sit down. I'll go and get him" she said, then invited us to the familiar living room, the leather couch, the magnolia walls with thin golden stripes, the clean fireplace mantle with an elegant fire burning in it.

We sat down on the leather couch and she left.

There was something strangely familiar, but it felt like it wasn't meant to be here. I looked closely around the room, the mantle above the fireplace. It didn't have pictures of my stepmother and my father, but there were books, the whole collection of *my* books.

"I recognise her, the maid. She was hard-working for her age when she came to work here" said my mother. There was a pause, "Is your Dad this wealthy Lei?" she asked me.

"Well, he opened a business when I was eight years old" I explained.

"Oh, ok", she replied in realisation.

We heard someone coming down the stairs, we stood up.

It was my father, the maid stood by the door. I looked at his face and he was still looking like his handsome self; he had many white hairs among the black. He sat down on the opposite sofa, "So, what are you here for?" he asked in his gentle voice.

"It's been a long time" my mother said, my father looked very confused.

"Taia?" he said after a long pause. "But... you didn't- you're meant to be dead?" he muttered in disbelief.

"Never say that, ok? Our family are survivors" she replied "I stayed with Lei after she found me!"

I turned to him and gave him a card bearing my identity. He looked at me and back at the card. "11 years have passed, it's true, we're home now" I said. My father stared at the card for a long time as if he could not believe what happened. He looked at me, "Lei... where did you go? I missed you so much" he said, his voice full of relief as his expression changed to a plead for forgiveness.

"It's nice to see you father. But I thought you knew where I was because I sent countless letters to you and you never replied!"

"You did? I never received any letters from you" he said.

I was very confused *how could he not be receiving any letters* I thought. "Where is *she, my step-mother*?" I asked.

"Oh, she left about a year after you went missing" he replied.

"Why?"

"Because I told her to" he said "I found out that she had hired a group of people to get you so she could take the prize money"

"Why did you put the posters up in the first place?" I demanded.

"I was desperate, she was the one who suggested it and she put them up before I even got a chance to think about it" he admitted.

"I'm sorry, but I couldn't go back to this house with her here" I said.

"It's ok, in fact I'm glad you went because you would have never met Grandma Xu or you would have never seen what the real world was like" he said.

"Yes, that is true" I agreed.

3 days later, we arrived on Hengsha Island. All my friends were standing in the clearing of our little hamlet.

My father looked bewildered. I cast a sideways glance at him, "Welcome home, father!"

Printed by Amazon Italia Logistica S.r.l.
Torrazza Piemonte (TO), Italy

17616762R00087